W9-CSV-427

"I'm sorry I've been so silly about this. It's strange that I should be telling you of all people."

He was staring hard at her. "Why do you say that, Hannah?"

"Well—you and I—I mean, we're miles apart, aren't we? In different worlds. Hank hinted that it was because of me that he didn't get a better table and we had to wait to be served—I must be a failure as a dinner companion. I wasn't exactly a success with you, was I?"

Valentijn muttered something forceful under his breath, then got up and walked over to where she was sitting and stood looking down at her. He seemed enormous, looming over her, and strangely reassuring, too. He said slowly, "You look pretty in that dress, Hannah."

She looked up at him shyly—she wasn't used to compliments, especially from elegant, self-assured gentlemen. She wiped away the last of the tears with the back of her hand and smiled at him. "It's new. I bought it just in case I got asked somewhere." She smoothed the soft folds of the skirt with a careful hand. "Well, at least I've had a chance to wear it."

She got to her feet and, as Valentijn didn't budge an inch, she found herself within inches of his waistcoat. He very gently drew her close and kissed her just as gently. "Good night, Hannah."

Romance readers around the world were sad to note the passing of **Betty Neels** in June 2001. Her career spanned thirty years, and she continued to write into her ninetieth year. To her millions of fans, Betty epitomized the romance writer, and yet she began writing almost by accident. She had retired from nursing, but her inquiring mind still sought stimulation. Her new career was born when she heard a lady in her local library bemoaning the lack of good romance novels. Betty's first book, *Sister Peters in Amsterdam,* was published in 1969, and she eventually completed 134 books. Her novels offer a reassuring warmth that was very much a part of her own personality. She was a wonderful writer, and she will be greatly missed. Her spirit and genuine talent will live on in all her stories.

THE BEST *of*
BETTY NEELS

HANNAH

TORONTO • NEW YORK • LONDON
AMSTERDAM • PARIS • SYDNEY • HAMBURG
STOCKHOLM • ATHENS • TOKYO • MILAN • MADRID
PRAGUE • WARSAW • BUDAPEST • AUCKLAND

If you purchased this book without a cover you should be aware that this book is stolen property. It was reported as "unsold and destroyed" to the publisher, and neither the author nor the publisher has received any payment for this "stripped book."

ISBN-13: 978-0-373-19899-3
ISBN-10:   0-373-19899-X

HANNAH

Copyright © 1980 by Betty Neels.

All rights reserved. Except for use in any review, the reproduction or utilization of this work in whole or in part in any form by any electronic, mechanical or other means, now known or hereafter invented, including xerography, photocopying and recording, or in any information storage or retrieval system, is forbidden without the written permission of the publisher, Harlequin Enterprises Limited, 225 Duncan Mill Road, Don Mills, Ontario, Canada M3B 3K9.

This is a work of fiction. Names, characters, places and incidents are either the product of the author's imagination or are used fictitiously, and any resemblance to actual persons, living or dead, business establishments, events or locales is entirely coincidental.

This edition published by arrangement with Harlequin Books S.A.

® and TM are trademarks of the publisher. Trademarks indicated with ® are registered in the United States Patent and Trademark Office, the Canadian Trade Marks Office and in other countries.

www.eHarlequin.com

Printed in U.S.A.

CHAPTER ONE

BABY VAN EYSINK had made up his tiny mind not to take his feed; all four and a half pounds of him was protesting, doll-like arms and legs waving and his small face puce with manly rage. The puce deepened alarmingly as his blue eyes, squinting with temper, stared up into the face above him. Not much of it was visible above the mask, only a pair of wide grey eyes thickly fringed with dark lashes, and a few strands of fine straight light brown hair which had escaped from under the starched cap, but the eyes had laughter lines at their corners and the voice, urging him to be a good boy and do his best, was soft and gentle, so that he allowed himself to be soothed, and his loud bawling became a series of protesting squeaks and snuffles until he squeezed his eyes tight shut and began to feed, reluctantly at first and then with growing enthusiasm.

His performance had been watched anxiously by the

girl sitting up in bed in the small hospital room. Now she spoke quietly, her English fluent but heavily accented.

'Hannah, you are a marvellous person, this is now three times that my little baby has fed from his bottle, and that after so many weeks with that drip thing. I am so very happy, I shall telephone his papa this evening and tell him and he will be happy too. Now we shall soon go home, is it not?'

'Not,' said Hannah. 'Well, what I mean is not for a little while longer—little Paul has to gain another pound and feed normally for at least three days. Besides, you're not quite up to looking after him yet, are you, Mevrouw van Eysink?'

'But there will be a nurse and when we are both quite well again, there will be a nanny.' The girl pulled herself up on her monkey rope and altered her position. 'I cannot wait for the moment when they will take this horrid thing from me!'

'Not long now.' Hannah's voice was as soothing as when she had coaxed the tiny scrap on her lap, now feeding noisily. 'You'll be as good as new once it's off; a few months' exercise and therapy and you'll be fit to dance at anyone's wedding.'

'Yours?'

'Heavens, no! Is your husband coming this week-end?'

'Yes, of course. Dear Paul!' The girl in the bed tweaked a lace frill straight and smiled to herself. 'I must not grumble, must I? I could have been killed, and worse, I could have lost my baby. It is a miracle that he was born, is it not?'

'It is. It's worth lying still in bed and then wearing a hip spica for a bit, isn't it?'

'Yes, oh, yes! Dear Hannah, you are always so sensible and reassuring just like Oom Valentijn…'

Hannah made a face under her mask; Oom Valentijn was quoted, praised and admired at least three times a day. He must be an uncle in a million, she decided and she was heartily sick of him. And a lot of good that did, for Mevrouw van Eysink had launched herself into a lengthy eulogy once more.

'I am devoted to him,' she declared, not for the first time. 'You see, I do not remember my father, and my mother is, how do you say? invalid, and I have no brothers or sisters—so I am a spoilt little girl, having my own way always until Uncle Valentijn comes to see me. I am four years old then and he is twenty-one, and he tease me and teach me to ride a pony and look after cats and dogs and ride a bicycle, and he does not allow me to cry when I fall off. He comes—he came—many times over the years, even after he is married…'

'Oh, is he married?' asked Hannah idly.

'Not any more. He was a young man then and it was an unfortunate marriage, for they found that they did not love each other and Annette went away with another man and there was a divorce…' She saw the look that Hannah gave her. 'You think that I should not be telling you all this? But I like you and you are discreet, and without you I should not have the little Paul and I must talk to someone, you understand? I love my Paul, but for Oom Valentijn I have a strong affection. Why, he even helped us to marry, for my mother did not find Paul rich enough, but Oom Valentijn told me to marry whom I chose and that money didn't matter, and he is right, although we are not poor, you understand. It is a pity that he is not married too, for he has a great deal of money and a beautiful house to live in.'

'Well, I daresay he'll find someone,' observed Hannah. There surely were plenty of girls around who would be glad to live in a lovely home and have all the money they wanted, even if they had to marry someone middle-aged to get them.

They lapsed into companionable silence, broken after a minute or two by Mevrouw van Eysink's small, excited shriek. 'Oom Valentijn!' She plunged into a spate of Dutch. Hannah didn't look round; for one thing little Paul needed one's undivided attention and for another, she wasn't all that interested. She knew exactly what he would be like—thick-set and balding and wearing pebble glasses, like the Dutch characters she had occasionally seen on TV or at the films: his opinions had been quoted so often now that she felt that she knew him very well indeed—and deadly boring he must be too.

She twiddled the teat in little Paul's mouth with a cunning hand because he was getting tired now and hadn't quite finished, but she had to look up when Uncle Valentijn walked past her to the bed, giving her a civil, 'Good morning, Nurse,' as he did so.

Her reply, equally civil, ended in a gasp. Uncle Valentijn wasn't running true to form. He was tall and his shoulders were enormous and he showed no signs of approaching middle age. True, his hair was iron grey, cropped unfashionably close, but his features, while not those of a young man, were remarkably handsome, with a high-bridged nose and a straight mouth and blue eyes—they were studying her now, briefly and with polite indifference, and Hannah flushed under her mask, glad that little Paul should give a loud burp and need instant attention.

Uncle Valentijn made himself comfortable on the side of his niece's bed. 'I'm sorry I couldn't come sooner, my dear,' and Hannah, liking his deep, rather slow voice, pricked up her ears. 'You seem to have made a remarkable recovery.' He bent and kissed one delicately made-up cheek. 'And just as pretty as ever. I saw Paul as soon as I got back—he sends his love and will be with you at the week-end.'

His niece beamed at him. 'He comes each week-end, but soon I shall go home, once I have this—this thing off.' She paused. 'Can we not speak Dutch?' She turned her head to look at Hannah. 'You will not mind, Hannah, if we speak in our own language? I am so tired of speaking yours…'

Her visitor turned to look at Hannah too and there was faint amusement in his eyes. 'Not in the least,' she said, and felt awkward and in the way.

'And how is my godchild?' he wanted to know, and crossed the room, to take the baby from her with a polite murmur of, 'May I?'

He knew exactly what he was about, she saw that at a glance, but then so he should. Hadn't Mevrouw van Eysink told her time and again that he was a famous paediatrician? Baby Paul was lucky; not only had he survived a bad motor car crash before he was born and then arrived two months too soon, but he had doting parents, who from all accounts were able to provide him with a more than comfortable home and as a bonus, Uncle Valentijn.

She received the infant back presently, laid him in his cot, collected up her bits and pieces, and with the advice that if her patient required anything she had only to ring the bell, she went. To her surprise, Uncle Valentijn got up to open the door for her.

She was waylaid almost at once by the willowy blonde who shared the staff nurse's duties with her on the Prem. Unit and as well as that, was a close friend.

'Hannah!' She put out a hand so that Hannah had

to stop. 'Hannah, who's that stupendous type who strolled in a little while ago—he's really something…'

Hannah interrupted her a little tartly. 'That's Uncle Valentijn.'

Her friend's large blue eyes popped alarmingly. 'But it can't be! He's fat and middle-aged and…'

'Well, I thought that's how he'd be—like that Dutch character we saw in that film a couple of weeks ago, remember? And I'd got heartily sick of him, anyway: Uncle Valentijn this and Uncle Valentijn that, day after day.' Hannah shifted her tray and prepared to move on. 'You know how it is, Louise.'

Louise giggled. 'Is he staying?'

'How should I know? He said "Good morning" and "May I" and the rest of the time they spoke Dutch. He didn't even look at me—I mean, not to see me, you know. People don't. I wish I had fair hair and blue eyes and a figure.'

Hannah spoke without a trace of envy for the girl with her, who had all those things.

'You're very nice as you are, love,' declared Louise. 'Have you had coffee? I haven't either, we'll pop down as soon as we've cleared up, shall we? There's nothing due until half past ten.'

'I'm famished,' observed Hannah. 'If only I didn't get so hungry then I'd diet.' She looked down at her small well-rounded figure and sighed, then muttered under her breath, 'Here comes the Honourable!'

Sister Thorne, the younger daughter of a viscount, no less, bore down upon them in a purposeful fashion which they had learnt to be very wary of. She was a large woman with a booming voice, constantly issuing orders and making sure that no member of her staff had time to do more than draw breath between one task and the next. She didn't look in the least like a member of the aristocracy, thought Hannah, watching her approach; she should have been as willowy and pretty as Louise, instead of which she was stout with a face like a well-bred horse, used no make-up and strained back her greying hair in an unbecoming bun. She was a splendid nurse, though, and made no bones about staying on duty when she should have been off if there was something on the ward she wasn't quite happy about. She expected her nurses to do the same, of course, and they did so without complaining, although whereas Sister Thorne, however late she was, was whisked away in some chauffeur-driven car to wherever it was she spent her evenings, the nurses had to run for a bus and spend the evening soothing their boy-friends' tempers because they'd missed the big picture at the local cinema.

She halted in front of Hannah now. 'You should have tidied away by now, Staff Nurse. I expect my nurses—my trained nurses—to set an example to the students. You've just left Baby van Eysink? I shall visit there next, I believe Doctor van Bertes is there, is he not? He will wish to see the notes of his niece's case. Be good enough to go to my office and fetch them and bring them to me there.'

She glanced at Louise, standing uneasily, wanting to go but not wishing to appear to be running away. 'Your cap is crooked, Staff Nurse, and you are wearing excessive make-up.' She sailed away and Hannah, with an expressive look at her friend, sped in the opposite direction, to shed her load in the dressings room and repair to the office and fetch the notes.

Sister Thorne and Uncle Valentijn were standing facing each other when she knocked and went into her patient's room, and she had the impression that they had been arguing. Well, she amended to herself, not arguing, neither of them were the type to do that, issuing statements perhaps and not agreeing in a well-bred way. Hannah handed her superior the notes and made for the door, to be arrested by the visitor's smooth: 'One moment, Staff Nurse Lang.' He gestured politely at Sister Thorne, who nodded graciously.

'I hear from both my niece and from Sister Thorne that it is largely through your efforts and patience that my godson is thriving. I—we are deeply indebted to you.'

Hannah, taken by surprise, blushed fiercely, mumbled that it hadn't been anything really and poised herself for flight. As she went she saw the look Uncle Valentijn gave her—amused, mocking and tinged with the indifference which she had detected in his voice.

A horrible man, she decided, nipping down the corridor, far, far worse than the Uncle Valentijn she had built up from her fertile imagination.

She was off duty at five o'clock, with two free days to follow, and she didn't see him again before she went off duty, half an hour late, because Baby Paul took twice as long as usual to finish his bottle.

'A pity you're off duty,' observed his mother. 'Uncle Valentijn will be back this evening—and you have days off too, haven't you?' She frowned. 'I do not like it when you are not here, Hannah, because Paul is sometimes not good, but of course you need your free time—I expect you have much fun.'

Hannah wrapped the baby neatly into a gossamer shawl and popped him into his cot. She said soberly: 'It's nice to have a change.' She bade her patient goodbye and fifteen minutes later, clad in a pleated skirt and a short-sleeved blouse, her small waist encircled by a wide belt, she went through the hospital doors into the dusty warmth of a London summer's evening. As she crossed the busy street, she didn't see Uncle Valentijn, sitting at the wheel of a powerful Bristol motor car, waiting to turn it into the forecourt of the hospital. He watched her with casual interest; an unassuming girl, he considered, but presenting a pleasing enough appearance. She should be walking down a country lane, he thought suddenly, not battling her way through London streets. The traffic lights changed and he swept into the hospital grounds, dismissing her from his mind.

Hannah joined the tail of a bus queue, waiting patiently while she allowed her thoughts to wander over the day behind her. She was glad that little Paul was perking up at last; it had been touch and go with him ever since his birth, but now it looked as though he was going to make it; another month or two of care and he would have caught up with his weight. She would miss him, and his mother too, for that matter. Mevrouw van Eysink was only a couple of years older than she was and although they came from quite different backgrounds they got on well.

She climbed on to her bus and was swept through the rather dingy streets, over the river and into still more streets, not dingy now but tired-looking backwaters, each row of Victorian houses looking exactly like the next. Hannah got off presently, walked down a side street and turned into another one leading from it. The houses here were just the same as all the others—shabby genteel was the expression, she decided, going down their length to the end of the row. Some of them were still occupied by only one family, but the rest had been converted in a ramshackle way into flats. From the outside they didn't look so bad, but the builders had skimped the paint and plaster inside and used cheap wood for the doors and windows, so that nothing quite fitted any more. She turned into number thirty-six and started up the stair-case the four flats shared.

She and her mother lived on the third floor, sand-wiched between an old lady who walked with a stick whose every tap could be clearly heard by those beneath her, and a young couple who were ardent dis-ciples of pop music, so that Hannah's mother never ceased to complain in her plaintive way about the noise. But despite Hannah's frequent suggestions that they should find somewhere else to live, both quieter and cheaper, she always refused. 'This is a good address,' she argued, 'and surely you don't grudge me that refinement? After all, your dear father was a rural dean and heaven alone knows how I have to scrape and screw on my miserable pension and the sacrifices I'm forced to make.'

Hannah, hearing it all for the hundredth time, had always agreed quietly and forborne to mention that a large portion of her own salary went to bolster up that pension. Her mother had never been able to cope with money; when her husband had been alive he had given her a generous allowance—too generous, as it turned out, for on his death it was discovered that he had been digging into his slender capital in order to pay it, and now, five years later, his widow still considered that she should have the same amount to spend upon herself. And Hannah had said nothing; her mother was still a pretty woman, a fact which her mother frequently pointed out to her, adding the invariable rider that she could never understand how it was that she had such a very ordinary daughter. She always said it laughingly, making a little joke out of it, but to Hannah, very conscious of her ordinary face and small, slightly plump person, it was not a joke.

Her mother's voice, high and girlish and slightly complaining, greeted her as she opened their flat door.

'Hannah? You're late, darling. I'm afraid I haven't done anything about supper yet; this warm weather has brought on one of my wretched headaches…'

Hannah went through the narrow hall into the sitting room. Her mother was lying on a rather shabby sofa, one beautifully kept hand to her forehead. 'Don't bang the door,' she added sharply, and Hannah said, 'No, Mother. I'm sorry you've got a bad head. I'll get supper presently.'

She gave a small soundless sigh as she said it; she was tired and hot and hungry, and just for a moment she allowed her thoughts to dwell on life as it had been five years ago. She had been nineteen then, living at home and helping her father as well as coping with the major share of the housekeeping in the nice old house where they had lived. There had been a lot to do and plenty of time in which to do it and leisure to ride the elderly cob her father kept in the field beyond the house, or cycle round the lanes. She drove her father too and helped the old crotchety man who ruled the garden, and as though that wasn't enough, she cooked most of their meals, so expertly that guests would compliment Mrs Lang on her cook, to be answered by a charming smile and a murmured: 'Oh, we manage very well between us,' which left them with the strong and erroneous impression that she had spent hours in the kitchen turning out the delicacies on the table. Which wasn't true, of course, but Hannah never let on; her mother was selfish and dreadfully lazy, but she loved her, despite the rather tepid affection her parent accorded her.

Hannah stooped to kiss her mother and then went into the small kitchen to put on the kettle; she had missed her tea and if she was to get their supper she simply had to have five minutes' peace and quiet first. She took the tray into the sitting room and sat it on the little table in the window, then sat herself down on a high-backed chair beside it.

'Been busy?' asked Mrs Lang idly.

'Oh, about the same as usual.' Hannah knew that her mother had very little interest in her work, indeed, she shuddered away from illness. 'Would you like a cup of tea, Mother?'

Her mother accepted a cup with a wan smile. 'Dear child, what a comfort you are—it's selfish of me, but I'm glad that you have no plans to marry.' Mrs Lang sipped her tea and took a quick questioning look at Hannah. 'You haven't, have you? I don't suppose you get much chance to meet young men…only doctors and students.'

'They seldom marry nurses, Mother. They can't afford to.'

'Oh, well, I daresay you'll meet some nice man one day.' Mrs Lang added with complete insincerity: 'I do hope so.' After a pause she added: 'And poor little me will have to look after myself.'

'I don't suppose I'll get married,' said Hannah gruffly, 'so you don't need to worry. What would you like for supper?'

And presently she went into the kitchen and made a soufflé and salad, and all the while she was doing that she wondered what it would be like to be married and pretty like Mevrouw Eysink, lovingly spoilt and petted and the proud mother of a little baby like Paul, not to mention a devoted husband rushing over each weekend with armfuls of gifts…

'Roses,' said Hannah, gazing unseeingly at the view of chimney pots from the kitchen window, 'hand-made chocs and diamonds…'

'What did you say, dear?' called her mother from the sitting room.

'Supper's ready, Mother.'

Hannah spent her days off in the usual way, slowly developed over the five years during which they had lived in London. At first they had made a point of going somewhere—an art gallery, a film they wanted to see, or a concert, but gradually things altered. Mrs Lang began to complain that she found the housework too much for her, even though Hannah did most of it in her off duty, and then, just for a little while, there had been the young man from the hospital pharmacy, who had taken Hannah out on several occasions. She hadn't wanted to take him home, but she finally gave in to her mother's request to meet him, and then sat and listened to her mother destroying, in the nicest possible way, the tentative friendship she and the young man had formed.

Not that her mother lied; she merely made it appear that Hannah was a dedicated nurse and moreover had promised her father when he died that she would live with her mother and look after her. Mrs Lang, without actually saying so, had led him to believe that she was suffering from something vague and incurable which necessitated constant loving attention. The young man hadn't given up immediately; he asked Hannah out once more and she had accepted. But when she had mentioned it to her mother that lady said without a moment's hesitation that she had invited several people to dinner on that particular evening and had relied upon Hannah to cook the meal. She had dissolved into easy tears, murmuring that she supposed that she was of no account any more and Hannah must certainly go out if she wished; the invitations could be cancelled. 'The first dinner party I'd planned for months,' she had finished plaintively. And the soft-hearted Hannah had hugged her and declared that she didn't mind if she didn't go out and she'd love to cook the dinner for their guests.

The young man didn't ask her out again; they still smiled and nodded at each other when they met in the hospital, but that was all. It hadn't been quite the romance Hannah had dreamed of, but it had been pleasant enough while it lasted, and somehow after that the little outings were discontinued. Her mother liked to watch TV in the evenings and do her embroidery or knit, and on the one or two occasions that Hannah had met friends from the hospital and gone to a cinema, she had been gently chided for leaving her parent by herself. So nowadays she turned the flat out, did the week's shopping and the washing and escaped thankfully to the library, where she spent a long time choosing books.

Very occasionally she went shopping for herself, but by the time their living expenses were paid and her mother had deducted her allowance from her pension, there wasn't much money over. Hannah, who loved clothes, had to make do with things in the sales and the multiple stores, but she had a splendid dress sense and a nose for a bargain and contrived to be in the fashion even if the clothes she bought were cheap.

There would be more money soon, she thought as, her days off over once more, she started back to the hospital.

She had been offered a relief Sister's post in a couple of months' time, and she was going to accept it. It would mean leaving the baby unit which she loved, but she had to get a Sister's post as soon as she could, and one couldn't quarrel with one's bread and butter. Perhaps later on, when Sister Thorne retired… Ten years' time— it seemed an age away; she would be thirty-four and settled into a rut from whence there was no escape— perhaps by then she would apply for her job.

She turned in at the entrance to the hospital, looking up at its mid-Victorian pile with an affectionate eye. It was a frankly hideous building, red brick and a mass of unnecessary turrets and balconies, high narrow windows which took the strength of an ox to open and shut and dreadfully out-of-date departments, yet she had a very soft spot for it. When, in a few years' time, St Egberts was moved to the magnificent new buildings across the river and already half completed, she would regret going. It had stood for hundreds of years where it now was, domi- nating the narrow city streets and rows of smoke-grimed houses, and it would never be quite the same again.

She had chosen to go back after supper. She could have stayed at home for another night and got up early and gone on duty in the morning, but it was always such a rush. She pushed open the main doors and crossed the entrance hall. Just as she was turning into one of the dark passages leading from it she was hailed by old Michael, the Head Porter.

'Message for you, Staff Nurse—Mevrouw van Eysink wants you to go to her room as soon as you come in.' He grinned at her. 'Very important, she said.'

Hannah had gone to poke her head through the small window in the lodge. 'Me? Why? Have I done something awful, Michael?'

'Don't ask me, love. She sounded excited like and said I was to be sure and keep an eye open in case you came back this evening. Her hubby's with her.'

Hannah frowned. 'I can't think of anything…' she began. 'I suppose I'd better go.'

She altered course, taking another passage which led her to the lifts. She wasn't supposed to use them, but there was no one about. She gained the Prem. Unit and slid inside the doors and peered cautiously round the office door. Louise was there, writing: the night nurses would already be busy settling their small patients for the first part of the night, making up feeds and handing out cocoa and sleeping pills to the mothers.

'You're late,' whispered Hannah.

Louise raised her pretty head. 'Hullo—Sister went off late and left me a mass of stuff to finish and of course we had an emergency in. I'm almost finished, though. I say, your Mevrouw van Eysink wants to see you.'

'That's why I'm here. Is something awful wrong?'

'Not a thing—all a bit mysterious and hush-hush; hubby's here, and the uncle was here this morning. I say, did you know that he's a famous paediatrician?'

'Yes, I knew. I'll nip along now—see you presently—I'll make a pot of tea.'

Mevrouw van Eysink was sitting up in bed and her husband was sitting beside her, an arm round her shoulders. He was a nice-looking young man and as he got up when Hannah went into the room, he was smiling widely.

'Hannah!' cried Mevrouw van Eysink. 'You do not object that we take your free time? But Paul must go back tonight and it is most important that we talk together.'

Hannah walked over to the bed, casting an eye over the sleeping small Paul as she went. 'Paul's all right?' she wanted to know.

'He has gained three hundred grams, but he does not like the other nurse—she is sweet and very efficient, but I think that deep inside her she becomes impatient and he knows it. He is a clever boy.'

Hannah agreed warmly. Baby Paul, arriving too soon into the world, had shown a good deal of spirit in just staying in it, let alone turning himself into a normal healthy baby.

'We wish to ask you...' began Mevrouw van Eysink, and nudged her husband, who went on:

'I am taking Paul and Corinna home at the end of next week, Hannah, and we want you to come with us. I have spoken to your Directrice and the doctors who have been attending and they say that it would be quite possible for this to be done, provided that you agree.'

Hannah's wide mouth had opened, so had her eyes. 'Me? Go with you to Holland? Oh, I'd love to!' She beamed at them both. 'But how?'

'Oh, you would be lent to us as a necessity to little Paul's health. Three weeks or a month. By then Corinna will be almost her own self once more.' He added slyly: 'Don't worry about your chances for the relief Sister's post; they're as good as ever.'

Hannah had forgotten all about that anyway. 'Oh, I'd be glad to come.' The smile faded as she remembered her mother. 'Mijnheer van Eysink, could I let you know for certain tomorrow? You see, I live with my Mother and she—she doesn't like being on her own; I'd have to arrange for someone…'

'Why, of course, Hannah, but I'm sure your mother would manage for a week or two with someone to help her. Is she ill or an invalid?'

'No, no, she's…she's just…'

Mevrouw van Eysink gave her a thoughtful look. 'Well, you talk to her, Hannah,' she advised briskly, 'and let us know tomorrow. Perhaps if she realised how important it is for little Paul to thrive for the next few weeks—and he does it better with you than with anyone else—I am sure she will fall in with your plans.'

Hannah, looking at the two smiling, happy faces, decided not to argue the point. She would have to think of something; she would be off in the evening and although she hadn't meant to, she would go home and talk to her mother.

She stayed a few minutes longer and then went over to the home, where she joined her closest friends over the inevitable pot of tea and told them her news. They were flatteringly surprised and excited, although one or two of them wondered privately if she would be able to persuade her mother to let her go—they had met Mrs Lang upon occasion and found her charming, pretty and quite ruthless when it came to having her own way.

Hannah went on duty in the morning, half prepared to find that the van Eysinks had changed their minds, but the moment she entered Mevrouw van Eysink's room, she was met with an eager demand for her answer.

She picked up little Paul and handed him to his mother before she replied. She would have to explain a little more about her mother, and she did it carefully, anxious that her patient wouldn't think that she was finding excuses not to go to Holland. 'So you see,' she finished, 'it's just a question of finding someone to be with Mother while I'm away, only it is a little difficult. She hasn't many friends and almost no family, and she would dislike a stranger.' She wrapped herself in the bathing apron and went to fetch Paul from Mevrouw van Eysink.

'We must think of something, Hannah.' Lost in thought, Mevrouw van Eysink nibbled at a beautifully manicured finger. 'I think perhaps I know what to do, but I will say no more at present.' She smiled brilliantly. 'You will see your mother this evening? Good, then we must hope, is it not?'

'I'm bound to think of something,' declared Hannah, more to comfort herself than anyone else. She bathed and fed Paul while his mother kept up a lively chatter about nothing in particular. And Hannah, her neat head bowed over the scrap on her knee, tried to think of someone whom her mother would accept as a companion for a few weeks. She could call to mind no one at all.

Presently, her two patients comfortable, she tidied everything away, and with the promise of sending coffee as soon as she could reach the kitchen, she picked up her tray and left the room. She was halfway along the corridor when she met Uncle Valentijn. He passed her with a coolly courteous good morning and a glance which didn't really see her. She doubted very much if he remembered who she was.

CHAPTER TWO

BUT HANNAH WAS WRONG. Uncle Valentijn greeted his favourite niece with a kiss, peered at the baby and asked: 'What have you been saying to your so sensible Hannah? She was fairly dancing down the corridor.'

He was told with such a wealth of detail that finally he put up a large, well-kept hand. 'Now let me get this straight. She's to go back with you? A splendid idea; she's been with you both since you were admitted, hasn't she? She seems a very calm young woman, hard-working and presumably unencumbered by boy-friends?'

'Well, you make her sound very dull!' declared Mevrouw van Eysink indignantly.

'She is not what I would call eye-catching.' He was laughing at her.

'Pooh, I'd rather have her than six of your Nerissas—lanky, self-centred…'

Uncle Valentijn's eyebrows drew together and the

smile disappeared. 'Perhaps I should mention to you that Nerissa and I have just become engaged.'

'Oom Valentijn, you haven't!—it's a joke!'

'No, it is time that I married again. I'm nearly forty, you know, *liefje*. Nerissa is a lovely girl, very chic and good company.'

'Is that what you want?' His niece's voice was quite shrill. 'Don't you want to love someone and be loved and give you a nice family?'

He got up and walked over to the window. He said flatly: 'I used to think that I did. Nerissa and I suit each other very well; I think I am past the fine raptures of youth.' He added soberly: 'And I'll thank you to be courteous to my future wife at all times.'

He turned round and smiled at her, but his eyes were angry, so that she said weakly: 'Yes, of course, Uncle Valentijn,' and then to change the subject as quickly as possible, 'What shall I do about Hannah? Her mother—it seems she is likely to make it difficult for Hannah to come with us. Not that Hannah said so, but the nurse who relieves her told me that Mrs Lang is a very selfish woman; she is a widow and has been spoilt all her life. Hannah goes out very seldom, I am told, because although her mother is never unpleasant, she makes Hannah feel guilty. And I am sure that she hasn't enough money to get a companion, and even then her mother might refuse to have such a person. What am I to do?' She raised tearful blue eyes to her listener.

'You've set your heart on having Hannah, haven't you?'

'She saved little Paul's life when everyone else said that he had no chance, and she made me be brave. If anything should happen to little Paul now…'

'In that case we must think of something, must we not?' He turned round as a ward maid came in with the coffee tray. 'Leave it to me, my dear.'

Stowing her worries away behind a calm face, Hannah worked her way through her day and then took herself off home, reluctant to have to explain what her mother would regard as unwelcome news, and still vainly searching for some argument which her mother might agree to. Not that that lady would refuse point blank, nor would she rant and rave, but she would weep a little and point out that she led a lonely life and Hannah mustn't consider her, so that Hannah, with her too soft heart, would give in.

And Mevrouw van Eysink had made her promise to go and see her when she got back to the hospital, declaring dramatically that she wouldn't sleep until she knew if Hannah was to go with them or not, and because the staff nurse on night duty was a friend of Hannah's and would turn a blind eye to a late visit, she had agreed, which added yet another worry, for how was she to explain if her mother had made it quite impossible for her to go with baby Paul?

She made her way home with mixed feelings—reluctance to start an argument with her mother, and eagerness to get it over, and as luck would have it, the bus was dead on time and had never gone so fast. She found herself walking down the street, only a few steps from the front door, with not a thought in her head.

As she turned the key in the lock she was surprised to hear her mother's quite cheerful voice call: 'Oh, there you are! I was expecting you—come in and tell me all about it.'

Hannah advanced cautiously into the sitting room, to find her mother sitting in her favourite chair with, of all things, a tray with glasses and a bottle of sherry upon it.

'Whatever…?' began Hannah, quite at a loss.

Her mother smiled archly. 'I've had a charming visitor. Such a delightful man—Doctor van Bertes—an important figure in the medical world, I imagine. Your patient's uncle, and so anxious about the little baby. It seems you are the only nurse he cares to trust him with and he came to beg me to manage without you for a few weeks.' She smiled to herself. 'He quite understood that I needed someone to care for me and he fully appreciated the sacrifice I would be making, and he begged me— oh, so charmingly!—to allow him to substitute your occasional help with a very good woman of his acquaintance who would come each morning and see to the household, do the shopping and cook me a little meal. Of course, how could I refuse such a generous offer?' She added peevishly: 'I don't know why you couldn't have told me about it sooner, Hannah.'

'I didn't know, Mother. That's why I came home this evening—to tell you.' Hannah took a deep breath and tried not to sound eager. 'You agreed to Doctor van Bertes' suggestion?'

'That's what I've just said if you'd been listening.' Her mother's voice was sharp. 'Now you're here, I could fancy an omelette—but have a glass of this excellent sherry first. Doctor van Bertes sent me half a dozen bottles with his compliments and thanks.'

Hannah needed a drink. She sipped with appreciation while she brooded on Uncle Valentijn; a man of resource and a bit high-handed too—supposing, just supposing she hadn't wanted to go? She had said that she did, though, and Mevrouw van Eysink must have voiced her doubts to him. Probably he considered that she was incapable of arranging her own affairs. Which, she considered fairly, was perfectly true.

She drank her sherry, got a dainty supper for her mother while that lady reiterated her high opinion of Uncle Valentijn and presently took her departure. It was still fairly early and although she had had a cup of coffee with her mother she hadn't had her own supper, and although she was a sensible girl and independent she wasn't all that keen on going into one of the small cafés near the hospital. She could, of course, see what there was on the ward when she went to see

Mevrouw van Eysink. She sat in the almost empty bus thinking about clothes and should she wear uniform, and what about off duty and who was going to pay her, and had to be roused by a friendly conductor when the bus stopped by the hospital. She was still pondering these as she went up to the Prem. Unit, where she found her friend in the office, reading the report for the second time.

She looked up as Hannah went in. 'Hullo. Mevrouw van Eysink's waiting for you—says she won't go to sleep until you've seen her. You lucky devil, Hannah, going to Holland—I expect they've got pots of money and you'll live off the fat of the land. Why can't these things happen to me?'

'Well, you don't need them,' observed Hannah. 'You're getting married in six months and then you'll be able to do your own housekeeping and live off the fat of the land yourself.'

Her companion laughed. 'On a house surgeon's salary? You must be joking!' Hannah smiled because she knew she didn't mean a word of it. 'Can I pop along?'

'Yes, do—I've fed baby Paul and she's only waiting to see you before we tuck her down for the night.'

But it wasn't only Mevrouw van Eysink who was waiting, Uncle Valentijn was there too, the epitome of understated elegance. Hannah, seeing him, hesitated at the door. 'Oh, I'll come back later,' she said, and withdrew her head, to have the door opened and find herself taken by the arm and drawn into the room. 'We're waiting for you,' observed the doctor. 'Corinna refused to sleep, so perhaps you will tell her at once if you are going with her to Holland.'

'Yes—oh, yes, I am.' Hannah smiled widely at her patient and was quite unprepared for the sudden gush of tears from Mevrouw van Eysink. 'My goodness, have you changed your mind?' she asked. 'I can easily…'

'Tears of joy', declared Uncle Valentijn. 'She has been on tenterhooks.'

'Oh, well, it's all fixed,' Hannah gave him a considering look. 'Thank you, Doctor van Bertes, for— for persuading my mother, it was kind of you.'

His blue eyes, cool and amused, stared back at her. 'High-handed, I suspect, is the word you would prefer to use, but baby Paul must be our first concern. I hope that your mother is content with the arrangements which I suggested.'

'Oh, very—and the sherry.'

His mouth twitched. 'I'm glad, and I know that Corinna, once she has finished weeping, will tell you that she is quite content with matters as they stand.'

His niece blew her delicate nose and smiled mistily. 'Dear Uncle Valentijn, what would we do without you? Paul will be so pleased that everything is settled, and so easily too.'

Hannah caught the doctor's eye and said quickly,

'Well, I'll say goodnight. It's time you were asleep, and I'm not really supposed to be here.'

'Nor am I.' He bent to kiss his niece, looked briefly at the sleeping Paul and went to the door where Hannah was still standing. She hadn't expected him to come with her and she stood awkwardly before muttering again: 'Well, I'll be off—see you in the morning, Mevrouw van Eysink.' She added very quickly, 'Goodnight, Doctor van Bertes.'

He didn't answer for the simple reason that he went with her, striding down the corridor while she fumed, wondering how she could slip away into the kitchen and see if there was a slice of bread and butter to be had. She was still mulling over one or two quite unsuitable plans when he came to a halt outside Sister's office. 'Have you had supper?' he asked.

'Supper? Why, no, but—but I'm going to have it now.'

'Good, I'll join you—I'm famished.'

How to tell him that he would be expected to creep into the kitchen and hack a chunk off the loaf and if Night Sister had done her rounds, make tea?

'Well—' she began.

'What I should have said,' observed her companion smoothly, 'was will you join me?' And at her obvious hesitation, even more smoothly: 'I can perhaps give you some idea of what will be expected of you when you accompany my niece.'

Hannah was too surprised to speak for a moment,

but hunger got the better of all her other feelings. 'That would be nice,' she said sedately.

'Good. We're not too far from the Baron of Beef. I take it that you may stay out until a reasonable hour?'

'Midnight, but I wouldn't want to be out as late as that.'

The blue eyes gleamed, but all he said was: 'Naturally not—you're on duty in the morning, I presume.'

He swept her through the hospital and out into the street and into a taxi, where she sat very upright in the corner, unaware that in the dark he was grinning with amusement, but once in the restaurant, among the lights and crowded tables, she relaxed a little.

'I hope you are hungry,' remarked her host. 'I am.'

'Well, yes, as a matter of fact, I am.' Hannah essayed a small smile, wishing that he wouldn't look at her with a faint mockery which made her uncomfortable. And as though he read her thoughts the mockery wasn't there any more, only a kind smile. 'Good. Would you like a drink while we decide?'

She accepted a sherry because she wasn't sure what else to ask for and bent to the enjoyable task of choosing her supper. She had dined out so seldom that she found this difficult, and when her companion suggested artichoke hearts with vinaigrette dressing for a start, followed by tournedos Rossini with new peas and new potatoes, she agreed happily and with relief. He didn't consult her about the wine, though; she drank what was poured into her glass and enjoyed it, only asking after the first sip, what it was.

'A claret,' she was told, 'quite harmless and most suitable to drink with a steak.' He glanced at her. 'I don't suppose you have much opportunity to go out, Hannah.'

The sherry had put a different complexion on things, and the claret was improving it with every minute. 'No, hardly ever. When my father was alive we had people to dinner and we went out to other people's houses, but not to restaurants.'

'Ah, yes, your father was a rural dean, your mother was telling me; you must have had a pleasant life.'

'Oh, yes!' Hannah just stopped herself in time from pouring out her pleasant memories to him and went red at the thought. The Doctor eyed her over his glass and wondered what he had said to make her face flame. He hadn't met anyone quite so shy and stiff for years; certainly he hadn't been in his right mind when he had asked her to join him for supper. Now if it had been Nerissa, with her gaiety and clever talk— He frowned down at his plate and Hannah, seeing it and the faint boredom on his face, launched into what she hoped was interesting chatter. He listened courteously, answering her when it was required of him, and uneasily aware that she wasn't used to drinking half a bottle of claret and it had loosened her tongue past repair.

Hannah, happily unaware of her companion's thoughts, chatted brightly over her trifle, having a little difficulty with words now and then. It wasn't until she had had two cups of black coffee and they were in the taxi going back to the hospital that her usual good sense took over again.

She checked the flow of talk with such suddenness that Uncle Valentijn turned to look at her, but whatever he intended saying didn't get said, for they were back at the hospital and she was already opening the door. He leaned across her. 'No,' he said quietly, and got out and went round and helped her out. He told the driver to wait and walked with her to the doors.

'Thank you for my supper,' said Hannah, and swallowed. 'I'm sorry I talked so much—it must have been frightfully boring for you. I had a glass of sherry with Mother and then another one with you and all that wine, and I'm not awfully used to it.' She added, to convince him, 'I'm a very sober kind of person, really. I—I hope you won't think I'm not—not careful enough to look after baby Paul.'

He took her hand in his. 'Hannah, I think you are a most fitting person to look after my godson. I would trust him with you absolutely.'

She drew a deep breath. 'Oh, that's all right, then. I wouldn't like you to think I'm not to be trusted.'

'My dear girl, Corinna trusts you, doesn't she, and likes you? I am very fond of her and of her husband and I would go to any lengths to make them happy; their opinion of you is much more important than mine.'

A remark Hannah didn't much care for, although she wasn't sure why, only that it hinted vaguely that he didn't like her, or at least, didn't think her worth an opinion. She wished him a sober goodnight and went through the swing doors, her pleasure in the evening quite spoiled.

But a sound night's sleep dispelled her doubts and she went on duty with a light heart. It remained light until almost noon, when Uncle Valentijn paid a lightning visit to his niece in order to wish her goodbye, and Hannah, unaware of this and walking down the corridor with Paul's feed from the milk kitchen, was brought up short outside Mevrouw van Eysink's partly open door. For once her patient and visitor were speaking English and Uncle Valentijn's voice, while not loud, was very clear.

'Of course I have to go, my dear—you seem to forget that I have my work like any other man. I'll see Paul tonight and he'll make all the necessary arrangements, so you need have no worries on that score.'

His niece murmured and Hannah, judging it to be a good moment in which to enter, had her hand stretched towards the door handle. She dropped it to her side at the visitor's next words, though.

'Don't thank me, *liefje*, I must admit that I have spent more amusing evenings, and don't for God's sake let her loose on the claret; my head aches with her chatter!'

Hannah felt her face glow. She whisked round and went soundlessly back the way she had come, her face very white now. She was in the milk kitchen with her back to the door when she heard the doctor's leisurely stride pass.

'Beast!' said Hannah with feeling. 'Horrible man! I hope I never see him again, and when I do I'll cut him dead!'

She marched back again with her tray, her nice eyes flashing with temper, her face still very flushed, so that Mevrouw van Eysink exclaimed: 'Hannah, you look as though you have been fighting a battle! Your face is most red and animated.'

Hannah allowed her calm professional mask to slide over her outraged feelings. She said cheerfully: 'The milk kitchen's like a furnace, it must be the hottest day we've had this summer.'

Mevrouw van Eysink watched her while her very small son was changed, soothed and offered his feed. 'There is much to talk about,' she observed happily. 'You wish to wear uniform, Hannah?'

'Oh, I think so, if you don't mind—Paul sicks up quite a bit, you know, and besides, it's most important that he doesn't pick up small infections. If I wore a dress and got it grubby or something on it, there's always the chance that it might upset him.'

'I have seen you only once—last night, in your clothes. It was pretty, the pink dress you were wearing.'

'Marks and Spencer's with an expensive belt someone gave me for Christmas.'

'Uncle Valentijn has been here to say goodbye; he was sorry to have missed you and wished me to express the hope that he will see you again in Holland.'

And very nicely put, thought Hannah, considering it was a fib. She murmured: 'How kind. Your uncle was so good as to give me dinner yesterday,' and waited for the next fib.

Sure enough it came: 'Yes, he told me how much he enjoyed it.' Mevrouw van Eysink heaved a thankful sigh at having got that over and done with and rattled on: 'He is anxious to get home. He is engaged just within the last week or so to a girl I do not like very much. Her name is Nerissa and I find that silly, and she is tall and slim and always very beautifully dressed; she does not like babies or animals and I cannot think why Uncle Valentijn wants to marry her, for she will not allow him to keep his dogs, I am sure, and never, never will she have a baby…'

'Perhaps the doctor doesn't mind?'

'Not mind?' Mevrouw van Eysink's voice rose several octaves. 'He is a baby doctor, I told you, Hannah—he loves the little babies, and the children too, even when they are tiresome.'

She eyed her son, leaning over Hannah's shoulder and bringing up his wind just as he ought. 'Will little Paul be the right size by the time I have another baby?' she asked.

'Oh, lord, yes—he ought to catch up within the next six months. Are you ready to give him a cuddle?'

They made a pretty picture, Hannah thought; baby
Paul still looked rather like a doll and his mother, in
her silk lace trimmed nightie, was quite one of the
prettiest creatures she had ever met. 'How long am I
to come for?' she asked.

Mevrouw van Eysink touched the baby's bald head
with a loving finger. 'A month. That's not too long,
Hannah? You will not mind living with us? There will
be a lot for you to do, but we will promise that you will
have time to yourself. We live near Hilversum, in the
country, and if you wish, you can ride in the woods
there, and there are shops to visit and it is easy to go
to Amsterdam or Utrecht. There is a car you can
borrow, and also bicycles.'

'It sounds lovely,' observed Hannah. 'I love the
country and I can ride—and you don't have to worry
about me being bored or anything like that, because I
never am. Anyway, I'm going to look after Paul.'

'And I'm so relieved about that, I have wondered so
much what I would do if you refused to come. You will
live with us, of course, and you will meet some nice
people I hope, when they come to dinner with us. We
have many friends.'

A new dress, thought Hannah, something for the
evening, I wonder if they dress up or should I just take
a short dress—two. A long one as well. She decided
there and then to get one of each; it would mean
spending most of the money she had in the bank, for

really there hadn't been much over each month by the time she had contributed to the household and bought dull things like tights, toothpaste and shampoos.

'Do you have lots of parties?' she asked.

Mevrouw van Eysink's eyes shone. 'Indeed, yes—I will tell you…'

'I'd love to hear. I'll pop Paul back into his cot and it's time for your exercises; you can tell me while you're doing them.'

The unexciting tenor of Hannah's life changed during the next ten days or so. There was a passport to get, an interview with the paediatrician and a number of instructions to make quite sure about, the best of her uniform to sort out and pack, and by no means least, some clothes to buy. Her wardrobe was small but adequate and she augmented it now with a cotton skirt, a pair of slacks and a couple of cotton tops which would go with either; these were quickly enough chosen from the multiple stores. She took longer over the choice of an evening dress. It had to be something she could wear for several years; plain, yet elegant enough to hold its own among high fashion. She found what she wanted in a small shop tucked away in an un-fashionable side street; a silk jersey in a pinky mushroom shade, with a wide neck, swathed belt, and a flowing skirt which was full without being bunchy. It didn't cost as much as she had reckoned on, which left her free to choose between a pastel voile dress and a leaf green cotton, each so entirely suitable that she bought them both.

She spent as much of her off duty as possible with her mother, and was surprised at that lady's cheerful acceptance of her absence for a month. True, the companion Doctor van Bertes had undertaken to find was everything which could be wished for, and if their cosy chat was anything to go by when she arrived for an interview, Mrs Lang would have nothing to regret. There had been a bad moment though when she had let slip that Mrs Slocombe's fees were being paid by the van Eysinks. Hannah had protested at that. 'They're paying the hospital for me, and I'm getting my usual salary, Mother, we simply can't expect them to pay for anything else. We can quite well afford it for a few weeks.'

Mrs Lang had dissolved into tears. 'You know I rely on your money to pay the bills, Hannah.' She had darted an angry look at her. 'And I need every farthing of my pension this month, I simply must have some new clothes. I haven't had a rag to wear for months…'

Hannah forbore from reminding her that only the previous month she had gone to Harrods of all places, and bought two dresses both expensive enough to swallow up all her pension, and it was as well that she didn't, because her mother went on: 'I can't understand you being so selfish, Hannah—you've bought clothes for yourself.'

Unanswerable, even though, if she discounted toothpaste and shampoos and such like necessities, she had had nothing new since Christmas. Hannah had given in without another word. Somehow she would save the money and send it to Mevrouw van Eysink after she returned to England. Meanwhile there had been no point in worrying about it. Baby Paul was still the most important person to consider; he was gaining a little each day now, turning the scales at five pounds; weighing him had become a major highlight of the day.

But it wasn't only Paul Hannah had to attend, his mother, faced at last with the removal of her hip spica, became a bundle of nerves and it needed all Hannah's patience and resources to get her through the tiresome but painless undertaking. It was a tremendous relief when everything was finished, to find that contrary to Mevrouw van Eysink's firm conviction, she looked perfectly normal. Provided she did exactly as she was told, Hannah assured her, she would be as good as new in no time at all. Mevrouw van Eysink eyed her tearfully. 'Dear Hannah, you are very strong; how could I have endured this without you? It is a sad thing that Paul cannot be with me at such a crisis, and Uncle Valentijn also—they have never allowed me to suffer.'

'Well, the suffering wasn't all that bad, was it?' asked Hannah cheerfully. 'It was only because you didn't know what was coming next. Anyway, you can forget it all now and think about going home.'

'Indeed I will, but I must not forget so soon, it must be told to Paul.'

'And Uncle Valentijn,' prompted Hannah.

The departure and journey home was something of a royal progress. Mevrouw van Eysink borne away tenderly in a private ambulance from Holland, and her husband driving a powerful Mercedes with Hannah, holding little Paul in her arms and surrounded by every conceivable necessity for the journey, enthroned on the back seat. They were given a splendid send-off by various of the staff headed by Sister Thorne, and a number of friends of Hannah's hung from ward windows, giving her the thumbs-up sign and waving as though they would never see her again. And the journey went with incredible smoothness; Hannah, who hadn't been out of the British Isles, was all eyes at the Hovercraft they boarded at Dover. She had never expected such a treat, nor had she been prepared for the excellent lunch provided for her while Mijnheer Eysink, leaving her comfortably settled with little Paul, joined his wife in the ambulance.

And as for the baby, he behaved splendidly. True, he woke from time to time, howling for attention, to be ministered to and soothed back to sleep once more, so that Hannah didn't have much leisure to look around her until they had left the Hovercraft far behind and had been driving for some time, and by then they were at the Dutch border. They travelled at speed after that, never leaving the motorway until Mijnheer van Eysink said over his shoulder, 'That's Utrecht ahead. We go round the city and take the Hilversum road.' He sent the car past a slow-moving van. 'Is Paul all right?'

'He's fine, fast asleep, just as he should be. If it isn't very much further, he can have his next feed at home. He's been so good, bless him.'

'Thanks to you, Hannah. I hope he won't be too upset when we arrive.'

'Why? We can go straight…'

'Well, no—you see, there's such a welcome laid on for them both. When Corinna had her accident everyone was so upset; they felt sure that she wouldn't get better, probably be a cripple, and certainly that the baby would be lost to us. So you see they want to express their delight…'

'Yes, of course. Mevrouw van Eysink won't be too tired?'

Her companion laughed. 'Very unlikely; she's been lying quietly for hours and must be spoiling for some excitement. All the same, when we get there I want you to stay in the car with Paul until we've got her indoors and in a comfortable chair.'

'A good idea,' agreed Hannah, and sat silent as he turned off the motorway at last into a side road, running between trees. She could see water from time to time as the trees thinned and gave way to meadowland and then crowded down to the side of the road again as they went through an open gateway into a sanded drive. The house was round a curve and Hannah examined it eagerly as it came into sight. It was a villa of a very substantial size, its roof a mass of gables, its windows framed with shutters and balconies sprouting on all sides. Mid-Victorian, she judged, built in the days when servants were easy to come by. But it looked comfortable, its paintwork pristine, the windows sparkling in the late afternoon sun, the gardens around it gay with flowers. Not quite her taste, but she was happy enough to like everything. 'What a lovely home for little Paul!' she exclaimed, and earned a delighted glance from Mijnheer Eysink as he brought the car to a halt beside the ambulance. 'We think so, too,' he told her. 'It's not beautiful or historic, but it's nice inside.' He got out. 'Stay here.'

He went across to the ambulance and Hannah watched as the front door was flung open and Mevrouw van Eysink was borne through it. She could hear excited voices from somewhere inside the house as she sat quietly, the sleeping baby on her lap, waiting until someone should come and tell her to join the party inside. There was a good deal of noise, there must be a lot of people there. She hoped Paul wouldn't wake, but it was almost certain that he would. Perhaps she would be allowed to take him somewhere quiet once everyone had taken a quick look at him. She smiled down at the small face and at the same time became aware that someone was approaching the car.

Uncle Valentijn.

'I might have known,' muttered Hannah, aware that annoyance at seeing him again was strangely mixed with a pleasant feeling of excitement.

CHAPTER THREE

SHE HAD TO ADMIT that Uncle Valentijn was a splendid figure. His enormous size would have ensured a second glance in any case, but his good looks and elegance certainly merited a third look besides. And not only that, he had an air of assurance—a man, she decided, who always knew what he was doing and why.

His greeting was pleasantly indifferent, so that her, 'Good afternoon, Doctor van Bertes,' was cool. He opened the car door and stood looking down at her for a moment. 'I'll have Paul, while you get out,' he suggested. 'Don't bother about that clutter, someone shall come and collect it and take it up to the nursery.'

She did as she was bid without speaking and then took Paul back into her arms. He stirred a little and she said rather anxiously: 'I don't suppose he'll stay sleeping…'

'Very unlikely, there's the devil of a noise going on, but you'll have to bear with it, I'm afraid.'

He led the way into the house, through a square vestibule into a large hall filled with people. It looked like the finale of a Ruritanian operetta, thought Hannah wildly; Mevrouw van Eysink was enthroned upon a large chair with her husband on one side of her and a formidable matron with a vast bosom on the other. That would be Granny, Hannah decided, and allowed her gaze to range over the other persons there. Family, she supposed; expensive hair-do's and prosperous-looking men smoking cigars, but mingling in with them were what she supposed were family servants; a thin woman in a black dress and print apron, several younger women in overalls, a young boy and an old man holding a trowel and lastly a rather pompous individual in a dark jacket and a bow tie.

Everyone looked round as she went in, but not to look at her or, for that matter, the doctor; all eyes were on the baby. No one had told her what to do; she made her way carefully to where Mevrouw van Eysink sat, and laid little Paul in his mother's arms, then retreated with discreet speed to the outer edge of the crowd. There was a chair against one wall, and before she sat down in it she took a quick peep at her patient. He and his mother made a delightful picture. Mevrouw van Eysink had chosen to travel in a delicate blue dressing gown, lavishly trimmed with lace. It set off her prettiness exactly and now, with Paul in her arms, she looked like a glossy advert in one of the classy magazines. And she was undoubtedly happy to be home. Hannah sighed without knowing it as she sat down. Almost immediately one of the women in overalls handed her a glass of champagne from her tray. Just what I need, thought Hannah; it had been a long day.

Someone was making a speech and everyone raised their glasses. Hannah raised hers and then put it down again. Uncle Valentijn, standing across the room and being head and shoulders above everyone else, enjoying a splendid view of her, was staring at her intently. Waiting for her to make a fool of herself, she had no doubt; if she chattered too much after a couple of glasses of claret what was she likely to do after champagne? She gave him a haughty look and turned her shoulder.

'Not drinking the toast, Hannah?' His voice was soft in her ear.

She turned to look up at him, her face red, her eyes flashing. 'Surely that's an unnecessary question from you, Doctor van Bertes? If claret makes me chatter, the risk of what I might do after a glass of champagne is too great to bear thinking about.'

If she had hoped to see him discomfited, she was disappointed, 'You were eavesdropping.'

'No, I was not. You have a clear voice and the door was open.'

'Then I must ask your pardon.' Only he didn't sound as though he meant it, and he didn't suggest that she should drink the champagne. Hannah, aware that little

Paul would probably behave like a cartload of monkeys after his angelic day, could have done with it, better still a large pot of tea…

The party was showing signs of breaking up and a wail from Paul sent Hannah through the guests, brushing aside Uncle Valentijn with no ceremony at all, but when she got to Mevrouw van Eysink, she was hindered by that lady insisting on introducing her to various people standing around her chair. Hannah smiled and murmured, and when there was a pause said urgently: 'He's wet, I expect, and he's hungry. Could I go somewhere quiet with him? He'll go to sleep again once he's been seen to and I'll bring him back.'

Mevrouw van Eysink looked relieved. 'Dear Hannah, of course! I have forgotten so much—I wished to tell everyone here about you, but there has been no time, and now I am a little tired…'

'You're going straight to your bed.' Hannah whisked round and caught Mijnheer van Eysink's eye. 'I hate to ask, but could your wife go somewhere and rest? She's tired out—a nap before dinner, perhaps? Will people mind? I mean, if they've come especially to see her and Paul…'

'Of course they will not mind. She goes this minute, and you will wish to take little Paul to his nursery.'

Baby Paul was shouting his tiny head off by now and explanations were hardly necessary. Hannah carried him upstairs behind the woman in the black dress and apron, smiling rather shyly at the friendly faces around her. But not at Uncle Valentijn, standing at the foot of the stairs, listening to the formidable lady; she sounded annoyed about something.

The nursery was at the back of the house on the first floor. Hannah, pausing only long enough to assure Mevrouw van Eysink that she would be along as soon as she had settled Paul, followed her guide through an archway and into a short passage. The nursery led from it, a large, airy room furnished with just about everything a baby could require. Leading from it was a bedroom, a bathroom and a little pantry, but she didn't stop to examine them. Paul by now was puce with temper and working himself into a splendid rage. Hannah changed him, laid him in his cot and thanked heaven that there was a feed still warm in the thermos. She was sitting in the comfortable little chair by the window, with him on her knee, gobbling it down, when there was a tap on the door and Uncle Valentijn walked in.

'Corinna asked me to make sure that you had everything you need. Paul is all right?'

'Fine now he's getting his supper. I'll top and tail him presently and put him down for a nap. I expect Mevrouw van Eysink would like to have him for a little while later on.'

'Yes, she asked me to say that she hopes you won't be too tired to have dinner downstairs. She's decided to stay in bed for hers. At eight o'clock—Paul should be settled by then.' The doctor strolled over to the window and looked out. 'When you have finished here I'll get someone to bring you a tray of tea. One of the maids will have unpacked for you. Don't bother to change this evening—there won't be any guests. I persuaded Corinna's mother to go home.'

'Oh, the lady with the…' Hannah stopped herself just in time.

'Just so,' agreed Uncle Valentijn blandly. 'She is a little—er—forceful, but has a good heart.'

Little Paul had finished his bottle and lay content, his small stomach full once more. Hannah wrapped him up snugly, said fondly: 'There's a good little man, then,' and popped him in his cradle again. All at once she felt forlorn and tired and uncertain.

Uncle Valentijn was on his way to the door and she said: 'Well, thank you for the tea, it was very kind of you…'

'You English and your tea!' He spoke with careless good humour. 'And don't thank me, Corinna asked me to see about it, that's all.'

He went away and Hannah busied herself getting the room to rights again, then went into the pantry to make up the next batch of feeds. Someone had got it all very well organised; everything she needed was there, presumably arranged for in advance. She had just finished when the tea arrived; delicate china set out on a silver tray with biscuits in a tin. She kicked off her shoes, took off her cap and sat down for half an hour's peace and quiet before going into her bedroom. Someone had unpacked for her, so she did her face and hair, put on her cap and shoes once more and walked back along the passage to Mevrouw van Eysink's room at the front of the house. That lady, nicely rested, consented to have a bath with Hannah's help and be returned to her bed, where she sat up in a fetching outfit against the great square pillows. 'I thought,' said Hannah, 'that you might like Paul for a little while. If I brought him along after you've had dinner; he's not due for a feed until nine o'clock...'

Mevrouw van Eysink agreed happily. 'And I will feed him, Hannah, and you can have your bath and get ready for bed if you wish and fetch him when you are ready. I am very tired, but I think you are even more tired.'

Hannah laughed and shook her head. 'Only a very little; it was a super journey for us. Paul was so good and he'll sleep like a top tonight.'

She didn't add that he would waken for his feed at midnight and three o'clock in the morning. It was just possible that Mevrouw van Eysink hadn't thought about that; in hospital there had been night staff as well as day staff, but now Hannah was going to do both jobs the clock round. Not that she minded overmuch; she was used to erratic hours and for all her smallness, she was strong. After a few days some kind of pattern would emerge and she would be able to take time off accordingly; until then she was quite content. She tidied the bathroom, wondering as she did so if Uncle Valentijn had gone yet; and was she to have dinner alone or with Mijnheer van Eysink? She thought probably the latter. She didn't really mind either way.

The gong sounded shortly after she returned to the nursery, but she hesitated about leaving Paul, even though he was sleeping like a cherub now. The same smiling girl who had brought her her tea knocked on the door and then held it open. 'I stay,' she said, and nodded reassuringly. After a moment's hard thought she added: 'I fetch…'

'Oh, good,' said Hannah, and added: 'I'll be back as soon as I can.' The girl didn't understand a word, but she nodded again and Hannah, with a last peep at little Paul, made her way downstairs.

There were several doors leading from the hall and as she reached the last step, Mijnheer van Eysink put his head round one of them. 'In here, Hannah.'

It was a pleasant room, well furnished and cleverly lighted. French windows were open on to the terrace beyond and a tray of drinks stood on a small wall table. Uncle Valentijn was still there, his back to her, bending over the bottles.

'Ah, Hannah, I trust little Paul is sleeping?'

She didn't like the blandness of his voice. 'Yes, Doctor van Bertes, I wouldn't be here otherwise.'

Mijnheer van Eysink gave her an amused glance. 'What will you drink, Hannah?'

She said pleasantly: 'Oh, tonic water with lemon, please.'

Mijnheer van Eysink frankly stared, and although Uncle Valentijn didn't look round she was pleased to see him stiffen.

'You're joking, Hannah,' observed Mijnheer van Eysink.

'No, as a matter of fact, I'm not.' She smiled at him so nicely that he grinned back at her and leaving his guest to pour the drink, invited her to sit down.

Hannah sat composedly, accepted her drink and took her part in the casual talk which followed. And over dinner, served presently in a large heavily furnished room, she continued to uphold the conversation, but only in a very modest way; answering questions put to her, agreeing politely with her companions' opinions, saying very little, in fact. She had already made up her mind to excuse herself the moment the dessert had been removed from the table with the plea that Mevrouw van Eysink would need her, but in this she was forestalled by that lady's husband, who got to his feet as the coffee was brought in, declaring his intention of having his with her and Hannah was to take her time before returning upstairs. Which left her with Uncle Valentijn, sitting opposite her, looking bored.

Hannah poured their coffee. She said recklessly,

'You look very abstracted, Doctor van Bertes, I expect you're thinking about your fiancée.' She smiled at him. 'Won't you tell me about her?'

'Why should you wish to know?'

She passed him the sugar bowl. 'Well, I expect you'd like to talk about her, wouldn't you?'

He stared down his arrogant nose at her. 'My dear girl, I cannot imagine what interest you could possibly have in my private life.'

She went slowly red, staring back at him. She had deserved the snub; she must have been mad, talking to him in that fashion. She drank her coffee, said quietly that it was time she returned to the nursery, and went upstairs, where, the maid gone, she busied herself getting Paul's feed ready. And an hour later, a sleepy little creature tucked under one arm, she made her way along to Mevrouw van Eysink's room, where she left him with his proud parents on the understanding that she should return for him in half an hour. She was glad of the little respite. She wrote to her mother, looked in all the cupboards and drawers to discover where her things were and made the feeds for the night. And half an hour had been enough. Mevrouw van Eysink, over-excited and tired now, was only too glad to be settled for the night. 'And mind you sleep,' admonished Hannah in a motherly voice. 'I'll come along about eight o'clock, shall I? Little Paul will be sleeping after his feed, then I can come after his bath and nine o'clock feed and help you get dressed and downstairs. There'll be someone to help?'

She was assured that there would be all the help she might need.

But even with the entire staff's cheerful help, she was to find her day a long one, and waking at midnight and again at three o'clock, although she slept soundly in between, hardly meant a good night's sleep. But it wasn't for ever, she told herself. Very soon little Paul would start sleeping through the night and as Mevrouw van Eysink got over her fear that her bones were going to break if she so much as turned her head, she would be able to do more for the infant. As it was, Hannah settled into a busy routine, taking her through her days with not much leisure but the satisfaction of knowing that both her patients were improving fast. And although it was a busy life, it was a pleasant one too. The weather, although hot, was no problem with a charming garden in which to wheel the pram, and willing hands to do all the chores save those to do with Mevrouw van Eysink and Paul.

Mevrouw van Eysink spent a good deal of her day sitting on the patio, taking her exercise when Hannah, the pram under a nearby tree, could help her. Mijnheer van Eysink came and went presumably to some office or other, so that Hannah saw him only in the evenings, and of Uncle Valentijn there was no sign. He had gone on the morning following his niece's arrival—and a good thing too, Hannah assured herself. After the first few rather hectic days, things were settling down nicely. She was even managing to get an hour or two to herself either in the morning or the afternoon—not long enough to go anywhere, but then there was no need of that. There was a splendid swimming pool at the end of the garden and Hannah, in one of the maid's swimsuits, spent her free time in it, secure in the knowledge that she was within shouting distance of the house if anything dire should happen. She swam well and there was an excellent diving board and long chairs in which to lie when she wanted to sunbathe. Life, despite her broken nights and rigorous routine, was quite fun.

It stayed fun for a week, at the end of which time little Paul had gained another pound and his mother was getting more active each day, to the satisfaction of the family doctor and the specialist who accompanied him. Hannah was given fresh instructions, complimented upon her nursing powers, while the hope was expressed that she was enjoying herself. Which, strangely enough, she was.

The day after the doctors had been was hotter than ever. Leaving mother and child sleeping in the cool of the trees beside the house, Hannah donned her borrowed swimsuit, wound her long hair into a knob on top of her head and made for the pool. Mijnheer van Eysink wouldn't be back until the early evening and the whole household was sunk into peace and quiet until half past three when tea would be brought out on

to the patio. She would have to feed Paul at three
o'clock, but that was more than an hour away. She
dived into the deep end and swam leisurely to and fro.
Presently she went to flop down on one of the loungers
round the pool and lay half asleep until a look at her
watch reminded her that there was barely time for one
last dive and swim before she must go back to the
house and change into uniform. She had done two
lengths of the pool and was on the last one when she
became aware that she was being watched.

Uncle Valentijn, in the finest of summer suitings,
elegant to the last button, was standing waiting for her.
And he wasn't alone. Hannah steadied herself on the
side of the pool and looked up at the girl beside him.
Not a girl, a very beautiful woman, exquisitely made
up, not a single golden hair out of place, and wearing
a thin silk sheath of a dress which made the most of
her very slender shape.

Uncle Valentijn said, 'Good afternoon, Hannah,'
and looked amused, but at least he picked up the old
towelling robe, found in some forgotten cupboard, and
lent to her with the swimsuit and held it out. Hannah
swung herself neatly up and out, very conscious of her
hair, loosened from its bun and streaming wetly all
over the place. She got into the gown, feeling plump
and dowdy and at a complete disadvantage. How like
Uncle Valentijn—he had done it deliberately, no doubt,
because this beautiful creature was undoubtedly his

Nerissa, and the contrast between them was quite laughable. That was if one could laugh, thought Hannah, shooting a look of fury at him and encountering mockery.

He said blandly: 'Nerissa, this is Hannah Lang, who is looking after baby Paul and Corinna for a few weeks. Hannah, my fiancée, Juffrouw van der Post.'

Hannah stuck out a damp hand and withdrew it again. Juffrouw van der Post had made no effort to take it, instead she slipped an arm into her companion's. She said, 'Hullo,' in a gentle voice which conveyed surprise, amusement and contempt nicely blended.

'We have come for tea,' observed Uncle Valentijn as he ran his eye over Hannah's shapeless, shabby gown. Hannah gathered its ample folds around her person. 'Then I may see you later,' she said in a tone of voice which hoped she wouldn't, and made off across the grass, followed by a faint tinkle of laughter from Nerissa and Uncle Valentijn's deep voice.

Fifteen minutes later, very neat in her uniform, she went to fetch Paul, to find Mevrouw van Eysink entertaining her guests from her chair and the infant, disturbed by the company, muttering to himself in his cot. Hannah would have whisked him away to the peace of the nursery, but his mother wanted to show him off first. 'Just a minute, Hannah,' she begged prettily. 'Uncle Valentijn hasn't seen him for a week and I'm sure Nerissa is longing to hold him.'

So little Paul, by now getting peevish, was studied and admired by his uncle and then handed to Nerissa.

Hannah, standing a little apart, watched. It should have been a picture to melt all hearts, and certainly send Uncle Valentijn's beating ardently; the lovely young woman holding the little baby. But Nerissa was uneasy; she held Paul as though he was a parcel of something nasty which might come undone at any moment, and he, knowing it, acted accordingly, going alarmingly purple in the face, screwing up his eyes and yelling his tiny head off. Nerissa forced a smile which turned to a look of extreme distaste as Paul dug his head into her shoulder and dribbled. For such a small baby he dribbled largely; she held him away from her with a cry of horror. 'Take it away!' she cried. 'It's dirty—my dress—my lovely dress!'

Hannah was already there, holding the now howling infant against her shoulder, soothing him gently. 'It'll wash out,' she pointed out kindly. 'It's only dribble— they all do when they're little, you know.' She could see that Juffrouw van der Post was beyond comforting, her lovely face was tight with rage. 'It's all very well for you,' she snapped in excellent English. 'No wonder you wear that hideous uniform!'

'It keeps me dry,' agreed Hannah cheerfully, and went over to Mevrouw van Eysink's chair. That lady was looking furious, but not with her small son or Hannah. 'I'll feed him and stay in the nursery for a little while, shall I?' suggested Hannah. 'He's so little, and people upset him.'

She had spoken softly so that the other two couldn't hear her, and Mevrouw van Eysink nodded. 'You wouldn't mind, Hannah? I'll have tea sent up to you.' She smiled suddenly. 'Dear Hannah, as soon as we can arrange something you shall have a whole day to enjoy yourself. You are a slave, and I do not like that—there should have been two of you.'

'I'm fine, and as long as you think I can manage by myself, I wouldn't want it otherwise.' They smiled and nodded at each other, then Hannah went indoors and presently, with Paul changed and fed and already dozing off again, she took off her shoes and her cap and made herself comfortable in an armchair by the open window and ate her tea. She was half way through her second cup and doing the *Daily Telegraph* crossword puzzle when there was a tap on the door. She had learned a few words of Dutch already, so she said very softly, *'Kom binnen'*, and looked round to see who it was.

She might have guessed. Uncle Valentijn, looming huge in the doorway. She put down her cup. 'Don't wake him up,' she hissed in a whisper.

For answer he came right in, stopped to look at the cot's occupant, then sat himself down on the low window seat by Hannah.

She put down the newspaper and pen with deliberation. She had precious little time to herself, he might at least let her have her tea in peace.

Her thoughts must have shown plain on her face. 'Please don't interrupt your tea, Hannah.' He crossed one very long leg over the other. 'I—er—felt I should explain about Juffrouw van der Post—she doesn't like babies or children very much. She's an only child herself and you know how it is…'

'No, I don't,' observed Hannah forthrightly. 'You tell me.'

'You are sometimes very…' he paused. 'I am a good deal older than you and…'

'I know, you're a consultant, used to having housemen and nurses hanging on your every word, and I'm only a nurse. If ever I should meet you on a ward, I promise you I'll be suitably servile.'

He opened his eyes wide, and she was astonished at their vivid blue.

'Hannah, you viper!' He added softly: 'Have you been at the claret again?'

'Indeed no, and I expect the minute you've gone I shall feel fit to go through the floor.' She added tea to her half filled cup with a hand which shook a little. 'Please accept my apologies, Doctor van Bertes. I was very rude.'

He smiled with such charm that she almost liked him. 'You're a nice change from the women I know,' he told her. 'But please forgive Nerissa; she feels awful about it.'

'Of course I forgive her. She'll feel quite differently when she's got children of her own.' She saw the rather bleak look on his face and wondered at it. 'She's got the most beautiful figure I've ever seen,' said Hannah, anxious to dispel that look. 'You must be awfully proud of her. I'm filled with envy…'

He got to his feet, all at once remote. 'You have a great many things which she has not,' he said soberly. 'Goodbye, Hannah.'

She said, 'Goodbye, Doctor van Bertes,' in a reserved little voice and didn't smile. Just for a few minutes he had been quite different, she had actually rather liked him, but now he wore that bland look on his face once more. She drank her cooling tea and thought how well matched he and his Nerissa were. She could just picture them married, their feelings wrapped in a layer of good manners, so that they would never shout at each other or throw things, or make it up afterwards. Maybe he was to be pitied; perhaps he still loved his first wife. Hannah ate the last biscuit and settled down to finish her crossword.

One of the maids came to tell her presently that Mevrouw van Eysink wanted her—and the baby, of course. Hannah gathered him up and went out on to the patio again. It was cooler now and she put Paul into his pram before she joined Mevrouw van Eysink.

She was told to sit down and help herself to an iced drink from the tall jug on the table at her elbow. 'They

have gone,' declared her patient. 'What a horrid girl is
Nerissa! I should not say this to you, but there is no
one else and if I do not say it, I shall burst! She called
my little baby It and she did not like him. She is not
the wife for my darling Oom Valentijn, who needs to
be loved very much and have children of his own. I
know him well, you see, and I feel that is right for him.
Instead of that he is to marry that—that…' She lapsed
into Dutch and then laughed. 'It is a good thing that
you do not understand me, Hannah, for I am being very
rude. Ah, well, there is many a slip, do you not say?'
She nodded and giggled. 'She has spoilt her dress—it
was a new one; she has many clothes, they are important to her.' She sat up. 'May we walk a little, Hannah?'

They strolled very gently up and down, Hannah
holding fast to one arm, while Mevrouw van Eysink
leaned on a stick. 'I do well, don't I?'

'Very. Another week or two and you'll be as good
as new.'

'Uncle Valentijn has been talking to me about you,'
and when Hannah's head shot round, startled, 'No,
nothing but good, I assure you. But he says that you
must have more time to yourself. He will arrange for
a nurse to come once a week after breakfast and stay
all day, so that you may go where you wish, and he
says that I am now well enough to have little Paul each
afternoon after his three o'clock feed, and that you are
to be free until six o'clock. My Paul comes home about

five o'clock, and there are women enough in the house if I should need help. So we will do that. I have been very selfish, Hannah, I have not remembered that you have to feed Paul twice in the night and that you are with him constantly each day. I am very sorry.'

Hannah said comfortingly, 'Look, you've no need to be sorry. I came with you to help you both, and I didn't expect a lot of free time—after all, I get a swim each day and the garden is so lovely there's no need to go out.'

'It is nice, isn't it?' agreed her companion complacently. 'But we shall do as Oom Valentijn suggests, for he is always right. The nurse will come on Saturday, because then Paul is home too and he can help with little Paul.'

'Thank you—only if it doesn't work we won't carry on with it. Little Paul is doing so well now, I don't want to risk him loosing weight or not sleeping properly—another two pounds and he'll be OK.'

'It doesn't sound much in kilos.'

'No, but it's enough. He's thriving now and he's got into a nice routine; before I go I'll get him started on four-hourly feeds and try cutting out the night feed—I think he'll be ready for it by then.'

'I do not wish you to go.' Mevrouw van Eysink sounded put out.

'Well, I'm not going yet. I've only been here a week—in three weeks' time you'll be feeling so much better yourself that you won't mind.'

'Is that so? Now, tomorrow do you think that we could go for a little drive? Claus shall take us and we could sit in the back with little Paul.'

Hannah considered. 'Why not—though it would be much nicer for you if you waited until Mijnheer van Eysink was free, then he could drive you and you could sit beside him and we'll sit in the back.'

'That would be better. You drive a car, do you not, Hannah?'

'Yes, but I'd rather borrow a bike, if I may? Or— or—you did say I could ride…'

'Of course you shall. There is a good little mare you shall have—she knows her way around here, so it wouldn't matter if you got a little lost.'

They both laughed, and then the shrill demands of little Paul sent them over to the pram.

Hannah didn't dare ride the following afternoon. First she must spy out the land a little; she borrowed a bicycle from the same obliging maid who had lent her a swimsuit, and pedalled in a wide circle round the villa. There were two villages fairly close by, she discovered, one much larger than the other, with a massive church, two shops, a café and a tiny bandstand in the centre of its small square. The second village was very much smaller, a mere handful of little houses gathered like chicks under a hen, in the shade of the whitewashed church in their centre. She liked it enormously, but it had no shop, no post office even, so she

cycled back to the other village, where she bought
stamps and chocolate and then went slowly back to the
villa, eating as she went.

It was lovely to be out again, wearing a cotton dress,
idling along pleasing herself. She sang in a rather small
wispy voice as she went, planning other afternoons like
it. She would ride on Saturday, but the following week
she might go into the city and look at the shops. She
had brought a little money with her and there would
be presents to buy. Not that she wanted to go home—
she was very happy despite her busy life. The van
Eysinks were kind and young and delighted with each
other and their baby and everyone else besides. It
would be nice, thought Hannah, wistfully, if she could
meet a rich young man who fell in love with her at once
and wouldn't take no for an answer and then carry her
off to a charming house full of cheerful people who
seemed to like looking after their employers. There
would be a huge garden, of course, and in time,
children, and she, of course, would have all the clothes
she could ever want, and in some mysterious way she
would become beautiful overnight. Like Nerissa. And
that reminded her of Uncle Valentijn—and how he
came to be part of her daydream, she told herself
crossly, she had no idea.

CHAPTER FOUR

SATURDAY CAME and with it the relief nurse, a girl twice Hannah's size with a round, pleasant face and a placid disposition. Hannah took to her at once and was surprised when Henrika told her in her heavily accented but fluent English, 'Doctor van Bertes say that you are a nice girl and I believe him; he does not tell the untruth.' She smiled widely. 'And you are nice, I think. And now you will tell me exactly what I must do, please.' And when Hannah had done that: 'And Mevrouw? Is there much to do for her?'

'Almost nothing,' Hannah assured her, 'only making sure that she does her exercises and walks a little.'

She said goodbye to her new friend, kissed the top of baby Paul's head and wished Mevrouw van Eysink goodbye for a few hours. She had already told her where she intended going, so that she could be found fairly quickly if she was needed, but she thought it unlikely; Henrika was obviously a very competent girl.

In slacks and a cotton shirt, her hair in a thick plait, she went to the stables, and five minutes later was ambling down the drive on the mare's back.

The mare was a little beauty, with just enough spirit to make riding her interesting. Hannah allowed her to go at her own pace along the lanes she had already explored on the bike; the small village first and then the larger one, where she had noticed a café—she would get something to eat there and water the mare. It was a cloudless morning and already hot, and the woods on either side of the lane were tempting. Hannah turned the mare's head and took a sandy path leading nowhere.

It was well after noon when she dismounted at the café, and she was pleased to see that another horse, a great powerful chestnut, was tied in the shade of the trees alongside; it showed that the café owners would let her water the mare. She left the two animals side by side, patted the mare's glossy neck and went inside. The café was quite small and dark after the bright sunshine outside, and it seemed rather crowded by reason of the billiard table in its centre and the ring of small tables arranged round the walls. There was a bar facing the door and she hesitated for a moment, a little shy of the curious glances being cast at her, then started towards it, to be arrested halfway by a well-known voice. 'Over here, Hannah,' advised Uncle Valentijn, sitting at his ease against a far wall, and when she stood, openmouthed and irresolute, got to his feet and pulled out the chair opposite him, so that there was really nothing she could do but join him.

He waited until she was seated before he sat down, lifting a finger to the bar owner as he did so. 'What would you like to drink, Hannah?' He smiled pleasantly at her. 'The iced orange juice is delicious.'

'That will be nice, thank you, Doctor van Bertes.'

'And you will be kind enough to have lunch with me? I drove over to see Paul and there are one or two things I should like to talk over with you.'

'He's not doing well?' asked Hannah instantly.

'As far as I can see, he is doing very well indeed, but there are one or two things…'

The orange juice came and she drank it slowly as he sat back in his chair drinking his lager, watching her. 'What things?' she asked, anxious to break a silence which was getting uncomfortable.

'Shall we eat first? There's not much choice here, but the *uitsmijter* is excellent.'

'Is that chestnut outside yours?' asked Hannah. 'How did you know where I was?'

'You were sensible enough to supply Corinna with your itinerary. Today is the only time in which I am free for a few hours…I hope you don't mind?' He smiled again and she almost smiled back at him. 'Would you like to try the *uitsmijter*?'

'Very well, as long as there aren't any onions in it.'

'Beef or cheese,' he told her seriously, 'on bread and butter, with fried eggs on top and a small salad.'

'Beef, please.' She added rather diffidently: 'Doctor van Bertes, it's—it's my free day, so you won't mind if I just eat my lunch and then go?'

His face was inscrutable. 'Certainly I shan't mind, although I must point out that I am going back to the villa by a particularly pleasant path through the woods. You have no need to talk to me, I shall ride in front and show you the way.'

She gazed down at the food put before her. 'That's very kind of you,' she mumbled, 'but I've all the after-noon…'

'This path takes all the afternoon.'

'Oh, well, isn't Juffrouw van der Post with you?'

'She is in Friesland on a weekend visit.' Uncle Valentijn sounded smooth, although she thought he was annoyed. She sampled the *uitsmijter* and said in a social sort of voice: 'What a pity—I expect you miss her.'

Her remark was ignored. 'The reason I wished to see you was to make sure that you have everything you might require for little Paul and that you are comfort-ably situated yourself. I am aware that you are working many more hours than you should; perhaps in two weeks or so we might hand over for longer periods to Henrika, but I should require your assurance that she and Paul get on well together before considering this. If you are entirely satisfied, then it should be possible for her to take over completely when you go. As it is, I have pointed out to Corinna that you must have another half day free each week at least.'

Hannah frowned at him. 'I'm very happy as I am,' she pointed out sharply, 'and surely it's for Mevrouw van Eysink…'

His voice was as bland as his face. 'You consider that I am interfering? I must remind you that little Paul is in my care and as far as I'm concerned he will be given every chance to become as healthy and strong as a full-term child. Paul and Corinna have asked me to do whatever I think is necessary for his well-being, and that includes making sure that his nurse doesn't become tired and irritable and impatient because she lacks sufficient leisure.' He finished his beer. 'Would you like another *uitsmijter*—or another orangeade? No? Then perhaps an icecream?'

He beckoned the proprietor and the man came with a little dish piled with icecream, lavishly decorated with whipped cream and chopped nuts. Hannah, who had had every intention of refusing to eat it—after all, he hadn't even asked her if she wanted it—allowed her liking for icecream to overcome her dignity. And while she ate it, Uncle Valentijn chatted pleasantly—about the surrounding countryside, the pleasures of Hilversum and Utrecht, the delightful weather, and the various bridle paths in the vicinity. He ended with the smooth hope that her mother wasn't missing her too much.

'It seems not,' said Hannah, savouring the last mouthful. 'She likes Mrs Slocombe very much.' She put down her spoon and added carefully, 'Thank you very much for my lunch. Now I'll be on my way again, I think.' She looked round the café looking for something which might be the Ladies!

'It's the door across the room—the left-hand one.' Uncle Valentijn spoke in a detached way, but his eyes gleamed with amusement.

Hannah thanked him politely and added, 'Goodbye, Doctor van Bertes.'

He was still there when she went back into the café, leaning up against the bar, talking to the owner. But he joined her at the door and crossed to where the horses were tethered. He said pleasantly: 'We go down this road for about a mile and then turn off into those woods on the right.'

Hannah was giving the mare a lump of sugar she had taken from the table.

'Please don't bother—I'm quite happy just riding along by myself.' She looked at him as she spoke and realised that she might as well be addressing the wall behind them. Uncle Valentijn was obviously a man who having made up his mind about something, had no intention of being diverted. She said reluctantly, 'Oh, very well, but I can't think why you're bothering...'

He swung her up into the saddle and got on to his

own horse. The face he turned to her wore a look of faint surprise. 'I can't think why either.'

They rode in silence for some minutes until Hannah, peeping at him, saw that the look of surprise had given way to a kind of consternation.

'You look rather worried,' she ventured. 'Is it little Paul?'

'No.' He spoke so coldly that she bit her lip and urged the mare to trot ahead. But presently he said in a perfectly ordinary voice: 'Turn on to the path now. Queenie knows the way, it broadens out presently.'

It was pretty under the trees and cool. Hannah sat easily in the saddle, her plait of hair over one shoulder, her cheeks pink from the fresh air and exercise. She looked pretty and the doctor cast her a sidelong glance as he urged his horse alongside her. They were going up a very slight incline and at its top he put out a hand and brought Queenie to a halt.

'If you look to your left, you'll see the villa to one side of those pine trees, and now look in the opposite direction—you can see Hilversum.'

'Where's Utrecht?' asked Hannah.

'To the south. It's too hazy to see clearly; in the winter when the trees are bare and the air is clear, you can see it easily enough. You must go there one day before you return to England. There are some good shops.'

'There's a museum I read about,' said Hannah who had forgotten that Uncle Valentijn was remote and mocking and didn't like her overmuch; indeed, at the moment he was a delightful companion. 'The van Baeren—there's some silver there, and paintings…'

'You are interested in silver? And old furniture?'

'Yes, although I don't know much about them. There's another museum, isn't there—the Central.'

'Yes. You have been reading up a good deal about the city, Hannah.'

She answered in a commonsense voice: 'Well, I hoped I'd have time to see something of Holland.'

They ambled on presently and the afternoon passed, to her surprise, very quickly. They were riding in a wide circle with the villa on the far side of the perimeter and they stopped again as they came out of the woods on to a narrow lane running beside a canal, and sat down on its bank, leaving the horses to graze while they sat, their backs against a conveniently fallen tree.

'Do you ride a great deal?' Hannah wanted to know.

'As often as I can. I live in the very heart of Utrecht, but I keep Charlie at Paul's place; it's a very short drive to and fro.'

Emboldened by his friendly manner, Hannah ventured: 'Your fiancée—Juffrouw van der Post—does she ride too?'

'She's a splendid horsewoman.'

'She looks as though she could do everything well.' Hannah had no idea how wistful her voice sounded. 'And she's quite beautiful.'

He gave her a cold stare. 'You will be telling me next what a lucky man I am.'

She reddened, because that was exactly what she had begun to say, but she met his chilly eyes with an honest look. 'Well, yes, I was, because that's what I think, but I expect you find that impertinent of me.'

'Yes, that's what I do think, Hannah. Tell me, have you a boy friend or fiancé or whatever you young things call it these days?'

'No.' She dimpled into a giggle. 'You sound very elderly!'

'I am a good deal older than you are, Hannah.'

'And Juffrouw van der Post?' she couldn't resist asking.

'You're being impertinent again.'

She felt suddenly impatient with him. 'Well, what do you expect? I didn't ask to ride with you, Doctor van Bertes—it was you who decided that.'

'So it was. I stand corrected. Let us cry a truce and discuss the view.'

Hannah looked at her watch. 'How long does it take to get back from here?' she asked. 'I told Henrika I'd be back punctually in case there was anything worrying her.'

Her companion smiled faintly; Hannah was a strange little creature, he thought. Usually the young women he took out were loath to part from him, and here was this rather plain, forthright girl anxious to be rid of his company. He got to his feet. 'Two hours if we don't hurry overmuch. Would you like to be going?'

'If you don't mind—or if you want to stay longer you could point out the way…'

'I also have to be back in Utrecht very shortly after tea.'

They rode on in silence for some time, back in the woods by now, going along sandy paths. It was cool under the trees and Hannah felt a sudden regret that her day was ending. But there would be others. Uncle Valentijn had promised her that, and she didn't think, with all his faults, that breaking his word was one of them. They came to an old-fashioned finger signpost presently and Hannah exclaimed, 'Oh—Drakesteyn—that's where Princess Beatrix lived, isn't it?'

'Yes, although I suppose she has moved to the palace now that she has become queen. We take this path, it will bring us out on the road near the villa.' He glanced at his watch. 'There is a little teahouse along here, we have time for a cup of tea if you would like that.'

'Thank you, I should. That *uit-uitsmijter* made me thirsty.'

The teahouse wasn't little at all according to Hannah's standards and it was fairly full; girls in pretty summer dresses, men in open-necked shirts and slacks, a sprinkling of older people in expensive clothes. Hannah felt conscious of her elderly slacks and cheap shirt. As they dismounted she said hesitantly: 'I'm not really dressed for this kind of place, and my hair…'

'Perfectly all right,' she was assured carelessly as he ushered her inside.

It was rather more than a cup of tea. There were little biscuits, tiny cream buns and gorgeous confections of chocolate and whipped cream, decorated with glacé fruits and nuts. Hannah, a practical girl, decided that since she had been invited to have tea, she might as well make the most of it. She ate with appetite, polishing off two cakes with all the zest of a schoolgirl on half term holiday.

'Do you diet at all?' asked Uncle Valentijn.

She went bright pink. 'No—I ought to, oughtn't I? I'm plump and I expect I'll get fat if I'm not careful. I've tried once or twice, but I get so hungry. When I start putting on weight I shall have to diet.'

'I shouldn't bother; dieting makes life very dull. Have another cake?'

She shook her head. 'No, thanks.' She added shyly: 'Shall I meet you outside?'

He nodded casually, 'Very well,' and watched her make her way through the tables to the far end of the café. Despite her fears, he decided, Hannah had a nice figure and once or twice that afternoon he had caught himself wondering if she were pretty after all.

They reached the villa half an hour later and he wished her a perfunctory goodbye and when she started to thank him for showing her some of the country, he brushed it aside so impatiently that she stopped in mid-sentence and slipped away. Of course, now that they were back at the villa he would want to be shot of her—probably he regarded the whole afternoon as a necessary waste of time.

Henrika was waiting for her, sitting placidly with little Paul on her knee. 'He's been with Mevrouw van Eysink for a good deal of the afternoon and he took his feeds like a man,' she reported. 'Well, I'm off—I'm going out this evening, dancing. Have you got a boyfriend, Hannah?'

'No, I haven't.' Hannah smiled briefly to show that she didn't mind at all. 'I had a lovely day—thank you, Henrika. I hope you'll come next Saturday.'

'Sure I will. *Tot ziens*, then.'

The evening passed tranquilly. Hannah, trotting to and fro about her various chores, was surprised when the gong sounded for dinner. She joined Mijnheer van Eysink and his wife in the dining room, feeling odd man out, as Uncle Valentijn had gone. She wondered where he was and then roused herself to answer Mevrouw van Eysink's kind enquiries as to her day.

The week slid away, each day a peaceful replica of the last. Both her patients were doing well now; Mevrouw van Eysink was getting quite active, although she was still frightened of doing too much, but with Hannah's gentle patience was getting over that slowly, and as for baby Paul, he was growing under their very eyes, his cheeks nice and round and rosy, his arms and legs becoming positively chubby. Hannah, getting ready for bed on the Thursday night, sighed with content. Everything was going so well and she would be free again on Saturday. She set the alarm for midnight and was at once asleep.

It must have been about one o'clock, just as she was dozing off after giving Paul his midnight feed, when she woke suddenly aware that something was wrong. She was out of bed and bending over the infant even as she thought it. Her heart turned over at the sight of him; his small face was paper-white and pinched and he lay very still, not crying. She picked him up very gently and was almost relieved when he was sick, but the sickness was followed by screams of pain which wouldn't be quietened. Little Paul was ill, and she made a guess as to the illness. 'Intussusception,' said Hannah, out loud to reassure herself, 'or I'm a Dutchman.'

With the infant cuddled close she reached the phone on the nursery shelf and dialled the number on the paper fastened to the wall beside it. Uncle Valentijn answered almost at once.

'Hannah speaking.' She hoped that her voice didn't sound as frightened as she felt. 'Paul's ill—great pain, colicky, vomiting, very pale, rapid pulse.'

Uncle Valentijn's voice was reassuringly calm. 'His last feed?'

'Midnight—he took it all and went to sleep at once. I woke about five minutes ago and went to look at him. He vomited then and he's screamed ever since—all of five minutes.' She waited for him to speak and when he didn't: 'I've not taken his temp yet, but his pulse is uncountable and he's very white.'

'Any ideas?'

She said impatiently: 'It looks like intussusception…'

'Good girl! Now listen. I'll be with you in ten minutes; keep Paul in your arms, rouse someone to open the side door so that I can get in, and if Paul or Corinna wake, reassure them.' She heard him replace the receiver before she replaced her own and picked up the house telephone.

As Uncle Valentijn came soft-footed into the nursery Hannah wondered vaguely how he had managed to get there so very fast. True, he was wearing slacks and a cotton sweater and his hair was a little ruffled, but she didn't pursue the thought. She laid little Paul down on the changing pad and held him still while the doctor's large hands went to and fro over the very small stomach. 'You're quite right, Hannah— we'll get him in at once and I'll operate.' He glanced up at her. 'Give him to me, I'll go along and see Paul and Corinna while you put on some clothes. You can have three minutes.'

He was bending over the baby again, picking him up and then making for the door, and Hannah, who had quite forgotten that she was wearing only a nightie and couldn't have cared less in such circumstances, rushed into her room and flung on her uniform. She was ready in slightly less than three minutes, quite neat and tidy in her uniform, even her hair, which had been hanging down her back, roughly plaited and pinned under her cap. She emerged as the doctor returned, this time with Mijnheer van Eysink as well as the baby. Neither of them took any notice of her; she was handed little Paul while the doctor spoke earnestly to his father and she wrapped the still screaming mite in a shawl, picked up a handful of nappies and stuffed them into her pockets, caught up a box of baby wipes and stood waiting.

The doctor switched to English. 'I've been telling them both that it isn't as bad as it looks,' he spoke bracingly. 'I've done two today, both completely successful, just as this will be—it's a common condition, isn't it, Hannah?'

She took her cue from him. 'Oh, yes; and it's quite a small operation and it's marvellous how quickly the babies perk up afterwards.' She smiled at her employer. 'He's in the best possible hands, too.'

'Yours as well as mine,' snapped the doctor. 'I shall want you to stay at the hospital and nurse him, Hannah. We'll go if you're ready.'

She almost told him that she'd been ready for the last couple of minutes, but she quite understood that it was almost as important to reassure the young parents as it was to get little Paul to hospital. She followed him soundlessly through the house and out of the door while members of the household hovered anxiously. Someone else opened the car door and she got in with the still screaming infant; it wasn't the same car as last time, part of her mind registered the fact that it was a Bristol as the doctor started the engine. 'I shall drive fast,' he told her.

The understatement of the year! thought Hannah; she wasn't nervous and she liked speed and knew that it was vital to little Paul, but she had to admit to herself that she would be glad when they arrived at the hospital.

Which they did in almost no time at all. 'You'll follow me,' said Uncle Valentijn as he got out, opened the door, took the now strangely quiet infant from her and waited while she got out too. She nodded, took the baby back and went with him through the wide doors of the accident room. They were expected, he must have telephoned from the villa. A small group of people closed in round them as the doctor strode through into the hospital itself to where a lift, its doors already open, was waiting.

'You will come into theatre, Hannah, and be ready to receive Paul when I have operated. He will be placed in a side ward and you are not to leave him. You will be relieved for short periods when I consider it safe to do so.'

'Yes,' said Hannah, anxiously watching the small

white face. Nothing would make her leave little Paul until he was out of danger—there was always the chance that symptoms might recur during the first twenty-four hours after operating. She was very strong, she had no doubt that she would be able to stay alert and ready to act instantly should that happen.

The theatre block was modern, splendidly equipped and brilliantly lighted. What was more everything was ready for them. Obedient to the doctor's quiet order, she handed over the baby to a theatre nurse and was led away to get into theatre garb. The doctor and his assistant had already disappeared into the surgeons' changing room, and by the time she was ushered into the theatre, they were scrubbing up in the scrub room and baby Paul, looking like a very small wax doll, was lying on the table, the anaesthetist carefully checking before he started the anaesthetic.

Uncle Valentijn performed the operation with monumental calm and great speed. Hannah wondered how he felt about it; it was impossible to see his face, of course, and even if she had been able to, she doubted if he would have shown any emotion. At length he nodded to his assistant, watched while Theatre Sister applied the tiny dressing, stripped off his gloves and spoke.

'Hannah, take Paul and follow me.'

She had the receiving blanket ready; the still unconscious infant was laid in her arms and she walked carefully out of the theatre, following the doctor's broad back down a short corridor and into a small room. Everything was ready here, too. She tucked little Paul into his cot and supported his head while his uncle set up a paediatric drip, spoke briefly to his registrar, and then gave her his instructions.

For the remainder of that night and all the next day Hannah hardly moved from Paul's cot. Thinking about it afterwards she was a little hazy about what she had done and what she hadn't. Paul had needed constant attention the moment he became conscious again, and that had been soon. The drip had to be calculated to the exact amount to be administered, the fluid chart had to be dead accurate, too, and half way through the morning the continuous suction had to be stopped and two-hourly aspirations started. By the end of the day she had reported that there was nothing more to aspirate, and glucose water was started.

She was conscious of Uncle Valentijn coming in from time to time, and once the drip was down, the infant's father, looking as pale as his son. And every few hours or so she was relieved for a short time, just long enough to have a drink or a meal but never long enough to sleep. By midday she didn't want to sleep anyway, although she knew that once she had a chance to close her eyes she would go out like a light for hours. Uncle Valentijn, looking his age for once, had had little to say to her, although Paul van Eysink had taken her hand and shaken it over and over again. He had brought a case of night things for her too and she accepted it gratefully, enquiring after his wife and sending reassuring messages. They were, she felt in her bones, through the wood; baby Paul was beginning to behave like a baby again, another day and he would be able to take tiny feeds of milk and water. Towards evening her false energy began to flag and she had the sense to realise that she would have to tell Uncle Valentijn to replace her before the night started. But she had no need to do that; when he came prowling through the door he had Henrika with him, beaming all over her face, full of vitality and anxiety to please.

The infant was examined, pronounced in good heart, and Hannah was told to give her report to Henrika and take herself off duty until eight o'clock the next morning.

She looked up at the Doctor. He still looked tired, but at least he was as elegant as ever, and as calm. 'Not too far from this room,' she said stubbornly.

He smiled a little. 'You're a glutton for work, Hannah! The room next door has been got ready for you. Sister suggests that you have a bath and get ready for bed and someone will bring you some supper. In the morning someone will bring you breakfast. I hope you'll sleep soundly in between.'

So she gave a concise report to Henrika, took a look at little Paul and went to the single-bedded ward next door, where she obeyed him to the letter, mostly because

she was too soggy with sleep to think for herself. She
had eaten half her supper when she fell asleep.

She was called at seven o'clock the next morning,
made an excellent breakfast, and with nicely made up
face, neat hair and a fresh uniform, popped back into
the infant's room. He was better; there was no doubt
of it. Henrika gave a reassuring report and prepared to
go. 'I come again this evening—I am to come each
night until you take Paul home. What suddenness,
Hannah!' She rolled her blue eyes expressively. 'And
what good fortune that you discover in time. You do
not mind coming here?'

Hannah looked surprised. Now she came to think
about it, there had been no choice; she had just come,
she hadn't thought beyond that at the time.

'No, I don't mind.' she said. 'I'm awfully glad it's
you, Henrika.'

'Me also. I was fetched from my home; Doctor van
Bertes sent for me. He is a splendid man, but cold.'

Hannah agreed silently, although she only smiled in
reply. At least he had saved little Paul's life; presumably he wasn't cold where his affections lay. Left
alone, she set the room to rights, made sure that everything she might need was in working order, and settled
to the day's routine. Uncle Valentijn had already been,
he wasn't likely to come again for a few hours at least;
she filled in her charts in a neat hand and started to
prepare the next small feed. Paul woke up then and she

whisked him out of his cot, changed him and then cuddled him for a little while. 'You're a big, brave boy,' she told him softly, 'and you're getting better— we can thank Uncle Valentijn for that…'

'Uncle Valentijn must return those thanks to his hard-worked nurse,' said the Doctor as he came in. He bent over her to look at the baby. 'Do you think of me as Uncle Valentijn, Hannah?'

It didn't matter how red her face was, she was gowned and masked and nothing showed excepting her eyes. 'Well, as a matter of fact, I do—you see, Mevrouw van Eysink always called you that, I didn't know your name…'

'But you do now.'

'Yes. I can't call you Doctor van Bertes to little Paul, he wouldn't know who it was.'

He gave a crack of laughter. 'You have a sensible answer for everything, Hannah. I've got his mother outside; she promised to be quiet and not cry, and I shall leave her with you for half an hour.'

He went back to the door and opened it and Mevrouw van Eysink came in. She walked with a stick, but Hannah saw with satisfaction that she was moving much more easily. Hannah got up carefully. 'Hullo,' she said cheerfully. 'If you like to sit down you can give him a good cuddle—he's a great one for that.'

Mother and child installed, she turned her back for a few moments, busying herself with the charts.

Mevrouw van Eysink must have time to shed a few of the tears her uncle had forbidden. 'There are a few things for you to write up,' declared Hannah in a businesslike voice, and marched past the surprised Doctor van Bertes out of the door.

'Why out here?' he asked mildly, following her into the corridor.

Hannah gave him an exasperated look. 'If I were Mevrouw van Eysink and Paul was my baby I would be simply furious if I couldn't have him to myself for a minute or two.'

'I stand corrected.' He spoke lightly, but she was puzzled to see that same look of exasperation on his face again, so she added,

'I hope you don't mind, sir.'

'I don't mind—I should have thought of that, but I do mind being called "sir" by you, Hannah. Don't do it again.'

'Oh, sorry—we call consultants "sir" in England.'

'So they do here, or the equivalent of it,' and at her look of bewilderment: 'No, don't try and work that one out. By the way, Paul will be here for another three or four days, then he can go home. You'll be tied to him for twenty-four hours a day, you know that, don't you? But his mother will be able to have him for an hour or so each day—this has driven the last vestige of invalidism out of her, so give her as much to do as you think right. Henrika will spend each Saturday at the villa and possibly a half day as well.'

He stared down at her and then put out a hand and pulled down her mask.

'Much too pale,' he observed. 'We are all in your debt, Hannah, and I think we shall never thank you enough.'

She stood looking up at him; the corridor was empty and it was very quiet save for the vague subdued sounds of hospital life in the background. When he bent suddenly and kissed her she didn't move. She was so surprised that she didn't really believe it; it wasn't until he said in an interested voice: 'Now I wonder why I did that?' that she knew she hadn't dreamt it. She had nothing to say, only pulled up her mask and went back to Mevrouw van Eysink and Paul.

And her employer was so insistent on knowing every single detail of the last few days, that Hannah pushed the incredible little incident to the back of her head and concentrated upon telling her visitor about all the things she wanted to know. She expurgated it a good deal and didn't appear to notice the tears trickling down Mevrouw van Eysink's pink and white cheeks.

'Uncle Valentijn told me I wasn't to cry,' she said, 'and I said I wouldn't, only I hadn't seen him then, had I?'

'There's nothing like a good cry,' pronounced Hannah in a motherly voice. 'You'll feel heaps better now—besides, you've cuddled him and talked to him and in a minute you're going to give him his feed. He only has a drop at present, but it will be more tomorrow.' She nodded her neat head. 'He's getting quite greedy, bless him!'

Mevrouw van Eysink was fetched by her husband presently, looking a great deal happier and prettier than ever. 'I'm coming each day,' she declared. 'You won't mind, will you, Hannah?'

'Indeed not, but did Uncle Valentijn agree?'

Husband and wife exchanged a quick glance. 'Yes, he said I could if you had no objection.'

'Did he actually say that?' Hannah looked her surprise. 'Then come whenever you want to, Mevrouw van Eysink. I'll be here; Henrika takes over about seven o'clock each evening and goes early in the morning, so there's all day to choose from.'

Mevrouw van Eysink crossed the room and kissed Hannah. 'You're such a nice person,' a tear crept down one cheek, 'and when I think what might have happened to little Paul if you hadn't been with him... Dear, dear Hannah! One day I will say thank you.'

Hannah kissed her back. 'I'm glad I was there, too. See you tomorrow, then. Paul will love to have you.'

When the pair of them had gone, she sat quiet for a few minutes. Paul was asleep and it was just a little early to get his next feed ready. She went over her conversation with Uncle Valentijn, trying to understand why he should have kissed her so unexpectedly. As far as she knew, he didn't even like her.

CHAPTER FIVE

LITTLE PAUL made an uneventful recovery, so that for the second time he was brought home to a warm welcome, though rather quieter than the first one. Uncle Valentijn had been very firm about that. Beyond a brief visit from his formidable granny, and quick peeps from the devoted staff of the villa, he was left undisturbed. There were flowers everywhere, of course, and the telephone ringing constantly, but Hannah, once more installed in the nursery, took little notice of that; she had her hands full with her patient, who, small though he was, was rapidly regaining his strength. But so was his mother. Mevrouw van Eysink had grown up, from the rather spoilt, pretty girl she had been, and was emerging a much stronger character. She still loved clothes and the best of everything, and her husband had only to hear her wish for something to get it for her, but now she had little Paul. Until he had been taken ill, he had seemed like a very much loved doll, and she was still recovering from her shocking accident—now she seemed to have cast all that aside and Hannah, delighted with her new interest in the infant, took time to explain his routine to her. Henrika would be moving in in a few weeks now, but as she pointed out to Mevrouw van Eysink, it was as well to know as much about looking after a baby as possible.

'I should have learned earlier,' Mevrouw van Eysink looked quite sad, but only for a moment, 'but then I was ill, was I not, and not able to look after him, but now I feel so very well...'

'You've learnt a great deal,' Hannah assured her. 'You could look after him, you know.'

'Yes, yes—but, Hannah, you are not to go yet. First our baby must be just as he was before he was ill, and I think that is not yet.'

'Well, he soon will be—look at him!' They bent over the cot and little Paul squinted back at them.

Uncle Valentijn telephoned each day, not for the sake of conversation but merely to request a concise report from Hannah, and three days after they had returned he paid a lightning visit, during which his manner towards Hannah was coolly courteous, which left her wondering if she had dreamed the episode at the hospital, and when they had been back for a week he came again, this time with his beautiful Nerissa, faultlessly turned out in a dream of stunning simplicity, her golden hair brushed and burnished and beautifully dressed, her face expertly made up. Hannah found herself wondering if she minded being kissed, for surely that would spoil the delightful picture she made. Perhaps Uncle Valentijn didn't like kissing overmuch. She frowned; if her memory served her right, he'd had a good deal of practice at it. They came into the nursery together, and Hannah, with little Paul in her arms, stood quietly, waiting for someone to say something.

It was Nerissa who spoke. 'Oh, the darling little man!' she said winningly. 'How wonderful that he has recovered so well.' She smiled bewitchingly at Uncle Valentijn. 'Due to you, of course, Valentijn.'

'Due to Hannah,' he observed.

Nerissa shrugged: she hadn't spoken to Hannah at all, now she added: 'Oh, well, one expects nurses to discover these things.'

'No, one doesn't—they're human, like everyone else. It happened in the dead of night, when even the most vigilant nurse might be forgiven for sleeping.' He strolled across to Hannah and ran a finger down the infant's cheek. 'He's looking splendid. Is he taking his feeds? And gaining weight?'

He took little Paul from her and looked carefully into the sleeping face.

Hannah produced her charts and reports and he read them, sitting in the big chair by the window, the infant still on his knee, and Hannah, remembering her manners, asked Juffrouw van der Post if she would like to sit down.

The lovely blue eyes narrowed. 'No—we only came for a quick look. Valentijn, are you ready?—Corinna and Paul will be waiting for us.'

'Go on down, Nerissa—I have to read these first; I'll follow you in a moment.'

And when she had gone, two angry spots of colour on either cheek, he asked: 'Have you had your day off yet, Hannah?'

She was surprised. 'No—Henrika couldn't come; she's on holiday, but I don't mind in the least, I'm not overworked.' She gave him a very small smile because so often when she smiled at him she received only a cold stare in return. But this time he smiled back at her.

'No, but you are tied to this small creature, aren't you? Is Henrika coming next week?'

'Oh, yes, on Saturday.'

He didn't reply, only handed back the baby before walking to the door, and his goodbye was very casual, almost as though he had forgotten that she was there. After he'd gone Hannah remembered that he had already read the charts and report before telling Nerissa to join the others. She found it remarkable that he had made an excuse to stay behind; surely someone as beautiful as Nerissa merited constant attendance, especially from a man who intended to marry her?

Hannah fed Paul and tucked him up once more, then went to sit by the open window and write to her mother. The letters she had been receiving from her parent were surprisingly cheerful. Mrs Slocombe must be a paragon!

Her tea was brought to her presently and later, when Mevrouw van Eysink came to see little Paul and feed him, observing that Uncle Valentijn and his fiancée would be staying for dinner, Hannah made haste to ask if she might have a tray in the nursery. She had, she explained, a quite bad headache, due to the heat. She didn't like fibbing, but the prospect of sitting with the other four, very much odd man out, was more than she could stomach. Uncle Valentijn was bad enough, but to have Nerissa there too, with that faint superior smile, pretending that she wasn't there, was enough to ruin her evening. Mevrouw van Eysink, instantly all sympathy, said of course she could have a tray, she herself would superintend its contents. 'And why not go to bed early?' she advised. 'You can eat your dinner in your dressing gown, and then rest in bed with a book until Paul's evening feed.'

Hannah hadn't intended doing anything of the sort, but she could see that Mevrouw van Eysink wasn't going to take no for an answer. She promised she would do that and presently Mevrouw van Eysink went away to change for the evening. She still had her stick, but she was walking quite well now; her recovery had been remarkable. Of course it had helped to have an adoring husband and a delightful little son, not to mention the relations who were forever telephoning and sending flowers and the hosts of friends who called each day. They were a very popular young couple—and nice too, mused Hannah, making sure that her charge was asleep before she went to run the bath.

Mevrouw van Eysink had been as good as her word. Dinner, when it arrived, was delicious, and Hannah, in her dressing gown, her hair newly washed, and hanging down her back, ate it slowly. Paul was sleeping; his feed wasn't due for another hour and she wished just for a moment that she could have gone outside and strolled round the gardens in the cool of the evening. Instead she switched on the small TV, turned the sound very low and concentrated on it. There was an elderly, very learned-looking man holding forth and she had no idea what he was saying, but he made company for her. She wouldn't admit to being lonely but she was.

She called, '*Kom binnen*,' when there was a tap on the door. It would be one of the maids to take the tray, and she looked up with a smile, but it was Uncle Valentijn, the picture of masculine elegance, who came in.

'Corinna tells me that you have a headache.' He glanced at the TV. 'You shouldn't be watching that.'

Hannah, feeling at a disadvantage in her dressing gown and her hair anyhow, frowned slightly. 'I find it most interesting.'

Uncle Valentijn chuckled. 'Indeed? Now that surprises me, Hannah—he is discussing Dutch politics in his own language too.'

Hannah smiled then. 'Well, he's company,' she admitted, and wished she hadn't said it.

'You're lonely.'

She said too quickly: 'No, no, of course not.'

He crossed his legs, leaning up against the wall as though he had taken root. 'At your age you should be out dancing with some young man.' He sounded amused, and she flushed painfully, waiting for him to add, 'But what young man in his right senses would want to go dancing with a plain girl like you?'

He didn't, of course, but she had no doubt that he was thinking it.

'I don't know any young men here,' she reminded him; there was no need to tell him that she knew precious few in London either.

'Then we must do something about that, Hannah.' He spoke kindly, and fearful of being pitied, she said brightly:

'Oh, I'm quite happy as I am, thank you. If you came to see Paul, I'm afraid he's very fast asleep.'

Uncle Valentijn left the wall and strolled back to the door. 'I came to see you, Hannah,' he said as he went.

She puzzled about that, her letter home quite forgotten, but she could find no answer, only the unacceptable one that he didn't trust her and felt that he should keep an eye on her care of Paul.

Nothing could have been further from the truth. Uncle Valentijn, back in the drawing-room, gave his opinion, albeit casually, that Hannah might like to meet one or two people of her own age. 'She will have to stay another week after the date arranged—that makes two weeks still to go, and she has had very little opportunity to get out and about.' He caught his niece's eye and added hastily: 'Oh, I'm not blaming you, *liefje*, it couldn't have been otherwise with little Paul so ill and you not quite yourself yet. She has done a splendid job of work and deserves a treat of some sort, don't you agree? Nerissa, surely you know some young people who would take her along with them for an evening's dancing or something of that sort?'

Nerissa smiled charmingly, but her blue eyes held a very wary look. She disliked Hannah, which was absurd, since she was a complete nonentity as far as she was concerned, but she never lost an opportunity to impress Valentijn. She said with a pretty little movement of her hands, 'Why, of course I'll help. I know simply heaps of people, I'll find someone for her. Don't you think that just one young man would be best to start off with? If I brought him along one afternoon, what would be more natural than that he should ask her out for a meal? Could that be managed?'

'Yes, of course,' declared Mevrouw van Eysink. 'If Hannah does the six o'clock feed she could have all the evening, because I could do the nine o'clock one— as long as I know where she is…'

'We'll make sure of that.' Uncle Valentijn gave his

fiancée a grateful look. 'That's very kind of you, Nerissa—she's free on Saturday, isn't she?'

'Then I'll drop in tomorrow—don't worry, Valentijn, I'll arrange everything.'

She was as good as her word. Hannah, wheeling Paul's pram round the garden the following afternoon was surprised to see Juffrouw van der Post emerge from the house and come towards her. There was someone with her, and Hannah didn't have time to wonder at the disappointment she felt because it wasn't Uncle Valentijn, before she was greeted with unusual warmth by Nerissa, who hailed her as an old friend. 'Hannah, I've brought someone to meet you—I was telling him about you and he wanted to see you.'

Hannah halted and blinked at the young man who had accompanied Nerissa. He was a little on the short side and plump, with brown hair already thinning at the temples, his dark eyes were almost obscured by heavily rimmed glasses, and he had a straggling moustache.

'Henk van der Kampen,' said Nerissa in a cooing voice. 'Henk, this is Hannah, and I'm sure you'll have a great deal to talk about.' She smiled a self-satisfied smile. 'I'm going to chat to Corinna for half an hour.'

Left alone with the visitor, Hannah looked him over carefully. He was dreadful; she loathed moustaches and eyes that never quite met anyone else's look. She said politely: 'Do you live near here?'

He had an Adam's apple which jumped up and

down his throat, too. 'In Soest, close to Nerissa's home. So you like being a nurse?' He made it sound a very inferior occupation.

'Very much. What do you do? Are you a doctor?'

'Certainly not! I don't do anything.'

'How very dull,' observed Hannah briskly. 'Now if you'll excuse me, I like to take little Paul for an airing at this time.'

'I'll come with you.' He glanced round him. 'This is quite a pleasant little garden.'

It was all of four acres. She murmured: 'Charming!' and waited for him to talk if he wanted to and wondered meanwhile just what Nerissa was up to. She very much doubted if the tiresome man walking beside her now had ever expressed a wish to meet her... perhaps he'd been bribed...

She realised that he had been speaking and she hadn't heard a word.

She turned an enquiring face to his and saw that he was put out. 'I was asking you if you would care to come out to dinner with me on Saturday.'

She was too surprised to answer at once. Not for one moment did she imagine that he had taken a fancy to her, but he must be doing it for some reason. 'That's very kind of you,' she said politely, 'but little Paul needs a lot of care still. I know I'm free on Saturday, but I won't go any distance in case I'm needed.'

He grumbled at that and when she said it was time

she went indoors with baby Paul, he followed her sulkily and although she made conversation of a sort as they went, he barely answered her. It was a relief to reach the house and go inside, but the relief was short-lived. Mevrouw van Eysink and Nerissa were sitting in the hall and Nerissa said at once: 'Well, is it all settled? I'm sure you'll enjoy an evening together and Corinna says she will love to have Paul for an hour or two—I don't suppose she sees very much of him,' she added slyly. She looked at Hannah. 'You look as though an evening out would do you good, Hannah.'

'Probably it would, but I think I'd rather not go, thank you all the same.'

'Nonsense—you can be too conscientious. Little Paul won't know his own mother soon, you guard him like a dragon.'

Mevrouw van Eysink's pretty face pinkened with anger. 'That's not true! You can be very horrid, Nerissa! I don't know what we should have done without Hannah—we shall always be in her debt.'

Nerissa laughed and got to her feet. 'Oh, one forgets hospital and nurses once one has got away from them—besides, Valentijn asked me to try and prise you loose from Paul. Henk, you can fetch Hannah on Saturday—shall we say half past seven?' She kissed Corinna. 'We must be off—I'll pop in again in a few days.'

Mevrouw van Eysink and Hannah looked at each other as Nerissa's car disappeared from the drive.

'Hannah, I am sorry, but I must say to you that I dislike that woman very much, and to have her for an aunt is beyond anything. She was unkind, and I am sorry.'

'That's all right, Mevrouw van Eysink.' Hannah went on thoughtfully: 'But you know, she's right. Perhaps now that little Paul is better, I should go home, and if Uncle Valentijn asked her to prise me loose, he must think that too.'

Mevrouw van Eysink stamped her foot, then winced a little and Hannah sat her down in a chair. 'Don't worry, you've not done any harm—your bones are quite solid again, but they'll hurt a little if you do that too much!'

'Oh, Hannah, you're such a comfort! And you are not to go home—and why should Uncle Valentijn think that? Only the other evening—when they came to dinner, you know—he suggested that you might be lonely and that you should go out with people of your own age.'

Hannah stared. 'Did he really? Well then, I'd better go, hadn't I?' She added wistfully: 'Only I wish he hadn't got a moustache.'

They burst out laughing then and fell to the interesting task of deciding what Hannah should wear. The silk jersey, of course, she had had no chance to wear it and if she was wearing a pretty dress and the dinner was good it might make Henk more acceptable.

Saturday came quickly and with it Henrika, cheerful as ever, full of her holiday, exclaiming over little Paul's splendid recovery and very interested to hear that Hannah was going out that evening.

'But I'm going riding all day,' said Hannah, and presently got into her slacks and shirt and went along to the stables where the mare was waiting. It was a lovely day again, the heat was already shimmering above the fields, but she had chosen to ride in the woods, along the sandy bridle paths, and when she came to a clearing with a café to one side of it, she stopped and had sandwiches and lemonade and then rode on. She had looked up the route early that morning and she had a map with her—besides, there were plenty of people around. She found her way easily enough and got back to the villa in the late afternoon.

She was dressed and ready and had shown herself to an admiring Henrika and Mevrouw van Eysink, when Henk arrived, driving a Porsche sports car. Hannah tied a scarf over her carefully done hair, put the wrap Mevrouw van Eysink had lent her around her shoulders and went downstairs. It was a pity, but even in a pretty dress and with the prospect of a good dinner, Henk was going to be hard to swallow, but since everyone seemed to think that it would do her good, she smiled and greeted him in a friendly fashion and got into the car with a show of pleasure.

'We're going to Utrecht,' he told her. 'There's a restaurant there which you might like.' He sounded faintly patronising and Hannah made haste to assure him that she was sure of it, then set herself to be an agreeable companion for the remainder of the short drive. A very different one from her previous journey into Utrecht; Valentijn had driven in a masterly fashion and with a complete absence of fuss, whereas Henk swore impatiently at the traffic lights, pedestrian crossings and any car which overtook him. And when they reached the restaurant he assumed a bullying air, demanding another table, and not getting it, sending back the wine and complaining loudly about the service. Hannah wished herself anywhere but where she was. Henk's loud voice was attracting the attention of everyone around them and as far as she could see his complaints were quite unfounded; the restaurant was a splendid one, the waiters performing their duties with pleasant speed and the food, when it came, was delicious. She did her best, carrying on a conversation constantly nipped in the bud by Henk's sulky answers, and it was a relief when he called for the bill and hurried her out of the restaurant. As they got into the car he said grumpily: 'Well, that was a wasted evening—I've always had excellent service there when I've dined with other girls. You don't want to go dancing, do you?'

He had started the car without waiting for her to answer him, and dancing was the last thing she wanted to do. Obviously he was trying to blame her for what he considered had been poor service at the restaurant, although how he came to that conclusion was beyond her—unless it was because she had no looks to speak of and her dress was something off the peg—very pretty in its way, but she had soon discovered that the women around them had been wearing lovely dresses which had never seen a peg.

They hardly spoke on the return journey and Hannah sighed with soundless relief as she saw the villa lights as they went up the drive. He pulled up with a jolt before the front entrance and she opened the door and got out.

'Thank you for a very pleasant evening,' she said mendaciously, and was taken by surprise when he lunged forward and caught her by the arm.

'Well, don't I get a kiss for it?' he demanded.

She considered his bad-tempered face. 'No, I think not. In fact, nothing would induce me to kiss you.'

She pulled her arm free and started to walk up the steps to the door and his voice followed her. 'My God, Nerissa said you were a starchy miss, and how right she was! I'm damned if I'll do her any more favours!'

Hannah opened the door and went in, not looking back. It was quiet in the house and dimly lit. Henrika would have gone hours ago and Mevrouw van Eysink would have fed Paul and gone to bed herself. Hannah crossed the hall, and as she did so the drawing-room door opened and Uncle Valentijn came out.

'Did you enjoy your evening?' he asked.

'No,' said Hannah baldly, and made for the stairs,

but he put out a hand and caught hers in it and turned her round to face him. He looked at her for a long minute and she stared back, her eyes very wide to stop the tears; she had just realised what Henk had meant about doing Nerissa a favour—he hadn't wanted to take her out at all; he'd done it to please Nerissa—and why had she suggested it in the first place?

'Come in here and have some coffee,' invited Uncle Valentijn placidly. 'Little Paul's asleep—I've just checked.'

Hannah went with him without a word and found herself sitting in one of the high-backed chairs, a cup of coffee at her elbow and him sitting opposite her.

'I was afraid...' he began, and then: 'Nerissa told me this evening that you were going out with Henk van der Kempen—he's a lout, foul-mouthed, ill-mannered...I can't imagine why she should have thought that you two would get on well together. Why did you go with him, Hannah?'

It was no good keeping her eyes wide open any longer; a tear slid down her cheek. 'Well,' she explained, 'Nerissa said you wanted to—to prise me loose from little Paul, that I guarded him like a dragon and his mother didn't see enough of him...' She paused to swallow her tears and the horror of what she had said made her gasp. 'Oh, I'm sorry—I shouldn't have said that! Please forget it—I'm a bit upset; none of it is true.'

'You're right, Hannah, none of it is true. I have never asked anyone to prise you away from my nephew, it is the very last thing I would wish to do, and Corinna sees more than enough of him—she isn't quite fit yet, despite her smiles and laughter—and it is owing to your care that they are both of them as fit as they are.'

Hannah wiped away a tear with a finger and sniffed. 'I expect I misunderstood Juffrouw van der Post. I didn't want to go with Henk, you know, but they said you wanted me to.' She didn't see his lifted brows and frown. 'He shouted at the waiter and made a fuss and when we got back here he was angry because I didn't want him to kiss me.' She looked across at her companion. 'He's got a moustache, and I hate them!'

Uncle Valentijn didn't smile, although his eyes twinkled. 'I don't care for them myself, Hannah.'

'Oh—well, he said I was a starchy miss, and Ner...' she stopped.

'Go on.' His voice was very soft.

'I've forgotten—it wasn't important.' Hannah put down her coffee cup and sat looking at her feet. 'I'm sorry I've been so silly about it. It's strange that I should be telling you of all people.'

He was staring hard at her. 'Why do you say that, Hannah?'

'Well—you and I—I mean, we're miles apart, aren't we? In different worlds. It just goes to show,' she went on slowly, 'he hinted that it was because of me that he didn't get a better table and we had to wait to be served—I must be a failure as a dinner companion. I wasn't exactly a success with you, was I?'

Uncle Valentijn muttered something forceful under his breath, then got up and walked over to where she was sitting and stood looking down at her. He seemed enormous, looming over her, and strangely reassuring, too. He said slowly: 'You look pretty in that dress, Hannah,' and she looked up at him shyly; she wasn't used to compliments, especially when they were uttered by elegant self-assured gentlemen. She wiped away the last of the tears with the back of a hand and smiled at him. 'It's new,' she told him. 'I bought it just in case I—I got asked somewhere.' She smoothed the soft folds of the skirt with a careful hand. 'Well, at least I've had a chance to wear it.'

She got to her feet and as Uncle Valentijn didn't budge an inch, she found herself within inches of his waistcoat. 'I think I must go now. Little Paul will wake soon—he mustn't cry and disturb everyone.'

He drew her close very gently and kissed her just as gently. 'Goodnight, Hannah.'

She murmured something and slipped away, up the stairs to the nursery and her own room. There was a full-length mirror inside the clothes closet. She stood in front of it and stared at her reflection. The dress was pretty, but any woman would know at a glance that it was cheap and she suspected that Uncle Valentijn was man of the world enough to know that too. And as for her face—it was all right, she supposed, but it had no beauty that she could discover, and her hair, although long and fine, was a very ordinary brown. There was nothing there to attract a man—one man in particular, that was, and anyway, he was already attracted to the beautiful, hateful Nerissa. 'You're mad,' Hannah told her reflection. 'Men like Valentijn don't look twice at girls like you.' She turned away from the mirror and started to undress. It was funny to think that when she had first met him she hadn't liked him and now she loved him.

It was as well for her peace of mind that she didn't see him for several days, and when he did come, Nerissa was with him, all smiles and sweetness, cooing prettily over Paul's pram, and wanting to know, in her excellent English, when Hannah would be going back home. 'You must miss your friends,' she smiled at Hannah but her eyes were cold, 'and your mother—Valentijn told me how much she depends on you. It was very good of him to pay for a companion while you were away, but of course he is very fond of Corinna and she had set her heart on having you with her.' Her tone implied that she couldn't for the life of her think why. She bent over the pram and Hannah digested this piece of news as best she could—she had thought that the van Eysinks had engaged Mrs Slocombe and Uncle Valentijn had simply been on hand to arrange things for Corinna.

'The dear little baby,' said Nerissa, loud enough for Uncle Valentijn, talking to the van Eysinks close by, to hear. Indeed he did look a cherub lying there, wide awake, smiling a big windy smile. Hannah, possessed with a mighty dislike of Nerissa, lifted him up and held him out to her. He needed changing, she could see that by the flood of colour in his tiny face, and it wouldn't hurt the wretched girl to realise that dear little babies weren't always sweet-smelling dolls.

Uncle Valentijn was watching. Nerissa, her smile fixed, accepted her small burden, casting a furious look at Hannah as she did so and holding the infant as gingerly as a bag of broken eggs. The smile wobbled and disappeared and she was on the verge of angry tears when Uncle Valentijn crossed the lawn pretty smartly, took the infant from her and handed him back to Hannah.

'I think you are better equipped to deal with him at the moment, Hannah,' he observed with a cold calm which sent shivers down her spine. Now she had cooked her goose. The man staring down at her now with such displeasure wasn't the man who had kissed her. She put baby Paul into his pram and wheeled him briskly away into the house and carried him upstairs to the nursery. He was lying clean and sweet and cuddly in her arms when the door opened and Uncle Valentijn walked in.

'That was unkind, Hannah,' he observed without preamble. 'Nerissa knows very little about babies…'

Having cooked her goose she might as well eat it, too. 'Then it's time she did,' snapped Hannah. 'How on earth is she going to manage when she's got babies of her own, I'd like to know? A permanent nanny, I suppose, and half an hour after tea with spotless little creatures who don't even know she's Mum.' She stopped because her eyes were swimming with tears of rage at the very idea of Uncle Valentijn's children having such a parent…and he would be such a wonderful father…

'We aren't all alike, Hannah,' said Uncle Valentijn quite mildly.

She looked at him quite wildly. 'Oh, I know, but you see she won't change—having a baby won't make any difference, all she thinks of is…' She stopped again under his quelling eye. The silence which ensued lasted a very long time; presently she said in a small voice, 'I expect you'd like to sack me and I'll quite understand if you do, but I'm not going to say I'm sorry.'

'I have no intention of sacking you, Hannah, and you do not need to apologise; I'll—er—gloss it over when I see Nerissa.' He came a little further into the room and sat down. 'You're unhappy, aren't you? Do you wish to go back to London? I had hoped you would stay another week, but if it's important to you, then I think something could be arranged.'

'Do you want me to go?'

He leaned forward and took her hand in his. 'No, Hannah, I don't.'

'Henrika is very good with Paul, you know, and I must be costing Mijnheer van Eysink a lot of money.' She wasn't looking at him, but at little Paul, deeply asleep, so that she missed the tender amused look he gave her.

'You will hand over to her, of course, before you go. I'll see that she takes up her post here a couple of days before you're due to leave so that she will know exactly how you have been going on.' He was still holding her hand and she didn't like to take it away, as probably he had forgotten about it. 'What are you going to do with your free day?'

'Oh, I thought I'd go to Baarn and find a present for Mother; I'd like to see the town too.'

'Until what time does Henrika stay?'

'Oh, about six o'clock, so I have all day.'

He nodded, gave her back her hand and got to his feet. 'Well, I must go, I've a lecture to give this evening. You haven't seen round the hospital, have you, Hannah?'

'No, only the baby unit and the theatre. It's a splendid one, isn't it?'

'We think so. I must see if we can arrange for you to visit it before you go home. Could you not do your shopping in Utrecht and combine the two on Saturday?'

She couldn't imagine why he was being so nice. 'Yes, of course, but would it be convenient—I mean Saturday—won't there be a lot of staff off duty?'

'I imagine not. I'll let you know.'

He gave her a brief nod and went away, and Hannah sat for a long time thinking about him. She had behaved disgracefully and he had been more than kind about it, and she suspected amused too. Perhaps he would be able to make Nerissa smile too. A tear escaped and tumbled down her cheek and she brushed it away impatiently; she was weeping far too often just lately.

It was Friday evening before Mevrouw van Eysink told her that Uncle Valentijn had telephoned to say that Hannah could visit the hospital during Saturday afternoon. 'Two o'clock, Hannah—and Paul will drive you in. Uncle Valentijn says he'll arrange for you to be brought back afterwards.' Her pretty face was wreathed in smiles. 'Isn't that very nice? You will enjoy yourself, I think. You have had no fun since you came—if little Paul hadn't been ill, you would have had more freedom. You are not angry that we have worked you so hard?'

'Not a bit,' Hannah assured her. 'I've loved being here and I'm going to miss you all very much when I go.'

A ready tear filled Mevrouw van Eysink's eye. 'I also, but we must not think like that, I must say to myself that I am well again and so is my baby.' She smiled, happy again. 'Paul is so very pleased with us, and he is a good father too.' She kissed Hannah's cheek suddenly. 'And one day you will have a good husband also, dear Hannah.'

No, thought Hannah, if I can't have Valentijn, I don't want anyone else. And I can't have him. She smiled and said brightly, 'Oh, I expect so.'

CHAPTER SIX

IT WAS HOTTER than ever when Hannah got up on Saturday morning, with a blue sullen sky and no wind. She suspected a storm before evening and while she was bathing little Paul tried to make up her mind what to wear.

She hadn't a great deal of choice; she settled for a blouse and pleated skirt and a blazer to go with them, then if it rained she wouldn't look too silly, and if it didn't she could take the blazer off if it got too hot.

She changed as soon as Henrika came and got the bike from the garage and cycled down to the village to post some letters. She didn't know how long the visit to the hospital would be and probably she wouldn't have time to shop—besides, she didn't know how she was to come back. Perhaps someone would put her on the bus which passed along the main road half a mile away from the villa. She didn't intend to worry about it, just as long as she was back by six o'clock. She did her hair and her nails and made up her face again before lunch, which she had with the van Eysinks before Mijnheer van Eysink fetched the car and drove her into Utrecht.

At the hospital he got out too and when she protested that she could find her own way to the porter's lodge, said easily that he knew his way around better than she did and could show her where to go. The porter on duty smiled and nodded as they passed him and started down a wide corridor lined with massive doors. This was the older part of the hospital, Paul van Eysink told her, and used by the administration. As he spoke he opened one of the doors and ushered her inside. It was a large room, with a table in the middle, with a dozen chairs drawn up to it, and a number of leather armchairs scattered round. Uncle Valentijn was in one of them. He got up when he saw them and the younger man said: 'Here you are, Valentijn, dead on time.' And to Hannah, 'Enjoy yourself, Hannah.' He was gone before she could utter a word.

'You look surprised,' observed Uncle Valentijn.

Hannah drew a calming breath. 'Well, I am—I thought there would be a nurse…'

He only smiled. 'Where shall we start? The accident room, perhaps?'

They were busy there, but as he pointed out, Utrecht was a large city and served a good stretch of surrounding countryside. Hannah, silent at first, warmed under his guidance, and found her tongue again. By the time they reached the medical floor she was asking questions as fast as he could answer them. They finished in the baby unit, which she had never had the opportunity to explore when she had been there with little Paul. It was nice seeing the Sister again and having the leisure to look round her, and this being Uncle Valentijn's province, they took a long time while Hannah poked her little nose into every corner of the unit. At length she was satisfied and said rather guiltily: 'I've been ages! I'm sorry—I must have wasted your afternoon.'

'Not in the least, Hannah.' They were walking without haste down the stairs; when they reached the entrance hall she said quickly: 'Well, that was delightful. It's a splendid hospital and I'm so glad I've seen it properly.' She held out a hand. 'Thank you very much, Doctor van Bertes.'

He took the hand, but he didn't shake it. 'Oh, we haven't finished yet,' he told her lightly. 'There's something else I should like you to see before you go back. Is your shopping very important or could it wait for an hour?'

'It can wait,' said Hannah recklessly. This might be her last chance of talking to him before she went home and she wanted to treasure every minute of it.

'In that case…' He held the door open for her with: 'Over this way, then,' and led her across the courtyard to where the consultants' car park was. The Bristol was there; he opened the door for her and she got in, supposing they were to drive to another hospital he thought she might like to see. The streets were busy, full of shoppers as well as traffic, and Uncle Valentijn didn't hurry, sliding the car effortlessly through the centre of the city and then turning off into a narrow street with a canal down its centre, and lined with large old houses, their staid fronts gleaming with paint and polished brass, their outsize front doors ornamented with beautifully carved swags of fruit or flowers. 'This is lovely,' observed Hannah, craning her neck in all directions. 'Seventeenth century, I suppose, and huge inside, no doubt. Are they flats or offices?'

'God forbid!' said Uncle Valentijn with some vehemence, and drew up before a double-fronted mansion. Hannah gave him an enquiring look which he ignored. As he opened the door he said casually: 'A cup of tea after all that inspecting?'

The eager 'Oh, yes!' was tripping off her tongue before she could stop it, but she added quietly: 'I feel you've spent too much of your time on me already. I can get tea when I go shopping.'

'My time is my own, Hannah.' He uttered it in a nononsense voice and she didn't care to stand in the street and argue with him; she got out and accompanied him up the double steps to the front door, opened as they reached it by an immensely imposing middle-aged man who in reply to Uncle Valentijn's quiet question

answered him gravely, bade Hannah good day in a
dignified manner and stood aside for them to go in.

Inside Hannah stopped to ask: 'This isn't your
house, is it?'

Uncle Valentijn sounded almost apologetic. 'Yes, it
is. When it was first built some two hundred years
ago, it housed a large family and a horde of servants,
now I'm afraid there's only me.' He indicated the
imposing man. 'And Wilrik, of course, and his wife
and a couple of maids.'

Hannah was taking in the imposing hall with its
high plastered ceiling and panelled walls, its austerity
softened by the great bowl of summer flowers on a gilt
and marble wall table and the magnificent chandelier
hanging from the ceiling, but she hadn't the time to see
everything, for Wilrik had opened a double door and
Uncle Valentijn was saying something to him. She
went past him into a room which took her breath away.
Its vast walls, silk-hung in a rich shade of mulberry,
were hung with a great number of paintings in ornate
gilded frames and its ceiling, even loftier than the hall,
was delicately painted and echoing its colours was the
Aubusson carpet under her feet. Cabinets filled with
china, glass and silver were ranged round the walls and
interposed, nicely blending with the richness around
them, were comfortable chairs and sofas, as well as a
number of small tables.

'Do sit down,' said Uncle Valentijn, and pulled

forward a small rose-covered crinoline chair. And when she sat, he lowered himself into a great winged armchair opposite her. He added softly: 'Hannah, close you mouth, you look like a worried little trout.'

Indignation snapped her jaws together, but only for a moment. 'Well, really! I am not a trout, and if you expect me not to be surprised at all this'—she waved an expressive arm around her—'then you're much mistaken.'

'Do you like it?' he wanted to know.

'It's quite beautiful—I expect that if you've lived here for a very long time you don't notice it very much.'

He smiled. 'Probably not—until someone tells me about it. But I assure you that I like living here and intend to go on doing so.'

A neatly dressed woman brought in the tea tray and Uncle Valentijn introduced her as Wilrik's wife, Meta, and when she had gone: 'You be mother, Hannah.'

So she poured their tea, very carefully because the cups were very thin porcelain and the teapot was a beautiful silver one and very old. Uncle Valentijn fetched his cup and saucer, offered her a sandwich and went back to his chair. 'My former wife never liked this house,' he observed casually.

Her eyes flew to his face. 'Oh, is she…' She paused, not quite sure how to go on.

'Divorced—fifteen years ago. Don't you think that it's time that I married again, Hannah?' He put down his cup. 'I'm almost twice as old as you.'

'No, you're not,' she said quickly. 'I'm twenty-four.'

'And very young with it. For a long time I felt perfectly satisfied with my life, but I realise that it isn't enough.' He crossed the space between them and she refilled his cup, then said carefully,

'Well, you'll be all right now you're going to get married to Juffrouw van der Post; she'll look splendid in this house—she's very beautiful, you know.'

'Oh, very.' His voice was dry. 'And much in demand, too—she will have so many social engagements that there will be no time for her to look after the house.'

'Well, that's what you must expect if you marry someone as lovely and popular as she is.'

His voice was suddenly impatient. 'No, it's not what I expect. I expect a wife to be waiting for me when I come home, knitting cosily by the fire or helping the children with their homework, and it's only during the last few weeks that I've realised that.'

Hannah looked at him round-eyed. 'It's a bit unusual,' she ventured. 'I mean, for a wife to sit and knit all day…'

'I didn't say all day, indeed, I would do my best to see that she enjoyed every moment…' He shrugged broad shoulders. 'No doubt I seem an elderly fool to you, Hannah.'

'No, you don't,' her voice was quite shrill with vehemence, 'and I do know what you mean—to come home to your wife and children each evening and be glad to see them and know that they're glad to see you—like the van Eysinks.'

'They are very young.'

'And what's that got to do with it?' she demanded. 'I imagine one can love someone at any age.'

His face had assumed its bland expression. 'Indeed one can, Hannah.' He got up. 'Would you like to see something of this house before I take you back?'

Hannah got to her feet. No doubt he regretted talking to her like that; perhaps he and Nerissa had had a tiff and he was feeling wretched. She said in a quiet voice: 'Yes, I should like very much to do that, but don't let me keep you.' She glanced at the clock. 'It's after five o'clock and I expect you're going out this evening.'

'Yes, I am, but there's time enough.' He opened the door and they crossed the hall to another pair of doors opening on to the dining room—a magnificent apartment with panelled walls, two great windows draped in almond green velvet and a three-pedestal dining table in mahogany around which stood twelve Chippendale chairs; a bow-fronted mahogany sideboard stood against one wall and a standing corner cupboard in the same wood displayed silver and porcelain. The floor was polished wood, almost covered by silky carpets. There were gilt and crystal sconces on the walls and a bowl of flowers between the candelabra on the table. 'Super!' breathed Hannah, wishing to linger, but her host ushered her across the room and through a small door in the opposite wall into the room beyond, a smaller room, gay with chintz curtains and a crimson carpet. There was a round table in the middle of the room with six Regency parcel chairs, upholstered in crimson brocade, arranged round it, and a very beautiful Dutch walnut and marquetry bombe-front bureau against a wall with a shieldback walnut chair before it, and set close to the small burnished steel fireplace was a small winged armchair covered in tapestry work. It was a charming room with a pleasant air of cosiness which Hannah was quick to feel. She looked enquiringly at Uncle Valentijn, who was watching her, a little smile on his face.

'You like it? My mother always used this room for what she called her quiet moments. She did her accounts at this bureau and sat here sewing or knitting while I sat at the table and wrestled with my homework. My sister and brothers were younger than I; they were still in the nursery and my father seldom got home before six o'clock.'

So now she knew why he expected his wife to be waiting for him with her knitting or whatever and the children with her. She felt near to tears when she thought of Nerissa, who probably couldn't knit anyway and disliked children. She tried to think of what to say and decided to say nothing, instead: 'How many brothers and sisters do you have?'

'A sister and two brothers—they're all in Canada at

the moment, but they live in Holland. They are all married. I was a year old when my father was taken away to a concentration camp; he came home two years later and my sister was born two years after that.'

'Your mother?' Her voice was gentle.

'She died two years ago—you would have liked her, Hannah. She never quite got over my father's death… Strangely enough her elder sister is still alive; eighty and very spry for her age, I might add. We must contrive a meeting before you go back to England.'

He opened another door. 'As you see, the hall again.' He opened a door. 'My study.' He barely gave her time to poke her nose round it before he shut it briskly. 'The library…'

Another vast room, well lighted by two floor-to-ceiling windows, with rows of books climbing the walls and a gallery running round half way up with a small spiral staircase in one corner. The chairs were comfortable and there was room enough for a dozen people to sit there without disturbing each other.

'Whoever built this house must have had an enormous family,' Hannah commented.

'Twelve children, so I'm told and they all lived to a good age, which was something unusual in those days. My brothers and sister already have five children between them, and I daresay there will be more.'

'I like families,' declared Hannah. 'I expect that's because I'm an only one myself.' She caught sight of

the clock, an enormous Friesland wall clock hanging
over the hearth. 'Oh, heavens, it's almost six o'clock!
I'm keeping you from your evening. Thank you very
much for showing me your home, it's beautiful and I'll
always remember it.'

Uncle Valentijn made no demur but led the way back
to the hall where Wilrik, warned by some sixth sense, was
waiting to open the door, and this time he bowed slightly
and allowed a fatherly smile to illuminate his dignity.

Hannah worked hard at light conversation during
their short drive, and although her companion—whose
manners were very nice even though he could be
arrogant when he felt like it—made suitable replies,
she had the feeling that he was absent-minded.
Probably he was glad that the afternoon was over and
was impatient to get to his evening.

But it seemed that this wasn't so. At the villa he got
out and opened her door, then accompanied her inside.
Once in the hall Hannah put out a polite hand and
began her thank-you speech, but he didn't listen; he
took her hand, it was true, but not to shake, only to
hold, and when Paul van Eysink came into the hall,
wanting to know if she had had a good time and would
they both like a drink he still held it.

'I'll not wait now.' He glanced at his watch. 'If I'm
back in just over an hour?' He glanced down at
Hannah. 'Will that be long enough for you to do
whatever it is you do for little Paul and get changed?'

She looked at him, quite bewildered. 'Me?'

'You. I should like to take you out to dinner, Hannah.'

'Oh, would you?' She sounded so surprised that the two men laughed. Not bothering to choose her words, she went on: 'But what about Nerissa? Won't she mind?'

Uncle Valentijn's face assumed its bland expression. 'Why should she?' His tone implied that she might have minded if it had been anyone else but Hannah. 'We're only having dinner together, Hannah. Nerissa is in Paris for the weekend and I daresay she's dining out too—why should we be condemned to solitary meals when we are apart?'

It seemed an unnecessarily long explanation to Hannah, but she could see his point—besides, Nerissa had nothing to fear from her, had she? Now if she had been pretty and golden-haired and blue-eyed and beautifully dressed, she would undoubtedly have at least tried...

'Hannah?'

Uncle Valentijn must have said something and she hadn't heard a word; she really must curb her tiresome imagination. 'So sorry, I was thinking...'

Uncle Valentijn's eyes gleamed beneath their lids, but all he said was: 'Eight o'clock, then, Hannah?'

'Yes, oh yes, I'll be ready.' She gave him a wide smile. 'I'll go and see Mevrouw van Eysink—she might have other plans.'

'She hasn't,' declared her husband cheerfully. 'As

a matter of fact we're looking forward to a cosy evening and getting in a bit of practice feeding the infant, so don't come tearing back at ten o'clock, Hannah, if you put everything ready we'll cope.'

'You're very kind—all the same I'll just…' She hurried off, her head bursting with a variety of thoughts. 'Thank heaven I washed my hair this morning early!' she muttered as she went into the sitting room to find Mevrouw van Eysink.

Baby Paul was angelic. Hannah topped and tailed him, fed him and popped him into his cot, then set about her own toilette. There wasn't much time; a shower, the pink jersey and ten minutes spent doing things to her face and hair and she was ready with a minute to spare. Just the same, when she got downstairs Uncle Valentijn was in the sitting room, talking to the van Eysinks and looking like every girl's dream in his dinner jacket. He got to his feet at once. 'Good girl—punctual to the minute! We'll be on our way, I've a table for eight-thirty.'

So they weren't going far. Hannah didn't ask where but sat beside him in the Bristol, feeling happy and talking idly about anything which came into her head. 'How quickly the summer goes,' she observed, 'and it's been a lovely one.'

'Weatherwise?' It was asked idly.

'Yes, but workwise too. It was dreadful for Mevrouw van Eysink having that accident, but if she hadn't I would never have nursed her or little Paul.' She added, 'Or come to Holland.'

'Or worked round the clock and given up your free time without a murmur,' observed Uncle Valentijn drily.

'Oh, that didn't matter. I shall miss it all when I go back.'

'To hospital, or have you other plans?'

She shook her head. 'Oh, no—if I stay there I'll be offered a Sister's post sooner or later.'

'And is that your ambition, Hannah?'

'Not particularly, but it's better paid, you see.' She peered out of the window. 'Oh, it's Utrecht again. Did we come this way this afternoon? I think I've seen it before.'

He had slowed to turn the car into a wide street. He said deliberately: 'You came here with Henk,' and before she could reply parked the car, held the door for her to get out and tucked a hand under her elbow as the doorman opened the big doors of the restaurant.

Hannah wasn't too happy. She hadn't enjoyed herself with Henk, but as far as she could remember she hadn't told Uncle Valentijn which restaurant they had gone to. Probably he thought he was giving her a treat—which of course he was, she reminded herself, and anyway she was quite sure that he wouldn't shout at the waiters and however bored with the evening he was unlikely to tell her so to her face. But she discovered that this evening wasn't going to be like her disastrous outing with Henk.

They were shown to a table by the dance floor by the restaurant manager, a waiter was waved into attendance, drinks appeared at a murmur from Uncle Valentijn and the menus were produced.

Uncle Valentijn had hardly opened his mouth, but there was the head waiter bending deferentially over his shoulder, recommending something special on the menu, enquiring tenderly of Hannah if she cared for asparagus au natural by way of starters or perhaps an avocado pear with the chef's special dressing?

Hannah began to enjoy herself. It was delightful to be fussed over, and when she looked enquiringly at Uncle Valentijn he obligingly suggested that the asparagus was usually good and how did she like the idea of lobster Thermidor to follow. Hannah, who had never eaten it, liked the idea very much, and when the waiter had gone and she was sipping rather cautiously at her sherry, she said so, rather shyly. 'It's not a bit the same,' she told him. 'I mean, Henk just ordered the food and I—I felt…I should have liked to have chosen something for myself but I expect he thought I wouldn't know what to order.' She smiled happily. 'This is fun!'

'I hoped it would be, Hannah. Do you like dancing?' She nodded.

'Then shall we let dinner wait for a few minutes?'

It was a good sized floor but fairly crowded. Uncle Valentijn danced as she had expected he would, very well, and although she seldom had the opportunity of dancing, she was good too. They danced in silence and when the music stopped went back to their table and started on the asparagus.

'You dance very well,' observed Uncle Valentijn, sipping without fuss at the wine the waiter had poured and nodding his approbation. Hannah watched her glass being filled and when the man had gone said: 'Well, I know it's not claret, and it looks like champagne, I think, but it wouldn't be?'

Uncle Valentijn made a small sound which might have been a laugh. 'Why not? It is champagne, it goes nicely with lobster.'

'Oh, does it? You see, I don't go out very much, so I don't know things like that.' She took a sip and said sedately: 'It's very nice.'

'I'm glad you like it. Would you like to dance again?'

The lobster appeared within seconds of them returning to their table and Hannah, being served with polite dexterity, reflected on the pleasure of being treated as though she were important and to be pleased at all costs, and yet Uncle Valentijn had made no attempt to impress anyone or raise his voice. But then he didn't need to, she thought lovingly, and smiled widely at him. She was halfway through the lobster when she glanced up and found him looking at her and she paused, her fork half way to her mouth. He looked as though he were amused about something and she looked at her glass, wondering guiltily if she had had too much champagne and was getting chatty again. She asked: 'Am I talking too much? You're looking at me…'

'Hannah, I must beg you to forget that unfortunate remark I made. I fear that you have saddled me with it for ever and regard me as an ill-mannered ogre.'

'Oh, you couldn't be ill-mannered if you tried,' said Hannah kindly. 'Arrogant, yes, quite often, but always very polite with it, if you see what I mean. And you're not an ogre.'

'In that case we might dance again.'

It was midnight by the time they got back to the villa. The house was in darkness save for a lamp in the hall and another one on the landing above. Hannah went past Uncle Valentijn as he unlocked the door and stood aside for her to go inside, where she stopped. 'Thank you for my lovely evening,' she said softly. 'I'll remember it always.'

He loomed over her in the dim quietness. 'So shall I, Hannah'. And very much to her surprise, he went back through the door, shutting it quietly behind him, leaving her to wonder what she had said or done to send him away so very quickly.

She went on wondering while she undressed, cast an eye over the sleeping infant and got into bed, where despite the advice she gave herself to go to sleep at once, she lay awake, still wondering and going over every moment and every word Valentijn had said and she had said... She fell asleep finally, to wake a few hours later at little Paul's urgent twitterings.

'You sound like a hungry bird, but you gobble like a great giant,' she told him lovingly, 'and I wonder if you'll miss me when I've gone away?'

She studied his little plump cheeks; he was fast regaining his health and strength. 'You won't, you know,' she told him, 'and you'll forget me—Valentijn will forget me too.'

A slow tear slid down her cheek and landed on his small bald head and he stopped guzzling to stare at her from round blue eyes.

She saw nothing of Uncle Valentijn during the next few days. If he had gone away there was no reason for her to be told. At meals, when she joined the van Eysinks, the talk was of her departure and the arrangements made for it and for the arrival of Henrika, who would take up residence for two days before Hannah left. Mevrouw van Eysink had been to Utrecht for a check-up and had been pronounced very nearly as good as new, and much of the talk was of the holiday they were planning in the autumn. But not a word of Uncle Valentijn.

It was towards the end of the week, with Hannah's departure only five days away, that Nerissa came. Hannah was in the nursery making up feeds, checking little Paul's clothes and writing a careful list of instructions for Henrika when she arrived the following day. It had been raining and she would have to take the baby out later on; it seemed as though summer was going to slide into a wet autumn, although it was still warm. Sitting beside the open window, engrossed in her charts, Hannah didn't at first hear the voices below, but presently Nerissa's: 'Let's sit here, Corinna, and do please let us speak English. I am going to England with Valentijn very shortly and I must get a little practice,' set her upright in her chair. The right thing to do was to go away from the window, out of earshot, even to close the window, but Hannah, her ears stretched, had no thought for the correct behaviour the occasion demanded. Instead, she edged her chair a little nearer the window and stretched her ears even further.

'Hannah leaves in four days' time, does she not?' Nerissa gave a little laugh. 'You will miss her.'

Corinna's voice, much harder to hear because it was pitched lower, answered. 'Very much. We have worked her so hard and she has never once complained. She has had very little time to herself.'

Hannah was happily unaware of Nerissa's lightning glance up to her window, but she did notice that her voice seemed even louder. 'Oh, I daresay, but I'm sure in hospital she has to work much harder and in unpleasant surroundings. And she has had several days to herself riding—and then Henk took her out.'

'Why did you ask Henk to take her?' asked Corinna. 'He spoilt her evening. It is a good thing that Valentijn took her out to dinner as well as showing her round the hospital and taking her to his home for tea.'

There was quite a long pause. 'Oh, yes—I'd quite forgotten.' Nerissa was feeling her way carefully, but her hearers weren't aware of that. 'Dinner and dancing.' It was a statement, but Corinna regarded it as a question as Nerissa had intended. 'Oh yes—they didn't get back until after midnight.'

'So I heard. Valentijn said that he'd never spent such a long evening in all his life. She's not his type, of course, but he told me that he felt that he should give her a treat before she went back. Henk found her a dead bore, but of course he was too young to conceal his feelings; Valentijn is so good at that, I daresay the girl thought he was enjoying himself too.'

'I don't think you should say that,' said Corinna. 'Hannah is a dear girl and she has never once bored me.'

Nerissa laughed. 'Oh, my dear, you are so naïve! Any man would find her dull, especially Valentijn, but I will say this for him, he always does his duty without complaint. Such a pity that I had accepted that invitation to Paris, although as it turned out, he was able to get the business over without wasting an evening on her without having to forgo dinner with me.'

'Well, that doesn't sound nice at all,' declared Corinna crossly. 'Valentijn knows how much we owe Hannah.'

'Well, of course,' Nerissa sounded impatient, 'but don't you see that's why he put himself out. After all, he doesn't have a great deal of free time, and to give up almost all of a day to entertaining someone he couldn't care if he sees again shows how much he realises you like her. And he would do anything for you and little Paul, Corinna.' She added: 'He wouldn't tell me if they had champagne, but I'm sure they did—he wouldn't do things by halves.'

'Uncle Valentijn is the nicest man I know—after Paul, of course,' declared Corinna rather tartly. 'You're very lucky to be marrying him, Nerissa.'

Hannah heard Nerissa's tinkling laugh. 'Yes, aren't I? He's got everything—a heavenly house as well as that nice place in the country, much more money than I could ever spend, and a name in the medical world…'

'That isn't what I meant.' Corinna's voice sounded cold and angry. 'I meant that he was a nice person, kind and patient and warmhearted.'

'Oh, that too,' said Nerissa carelessly. 'Let's walk on, shall we, it looks as though it might rain, and I don't want to ruin my hair.'

Hannah sat like a small statue. Listeners never heard any good of themselves, she knew that, and it had been demonstrated to her very fully now. Since she was not a devious person herself, it didn't enter her head that Nerissa had set the scene and deliberately twisted the truth. She went hot and cold with shame imagining Uncle Valentijn telling Nerissa all about it and laughing too, never for one moment entertaining the idea that Nerissa, knowing nothing but the fact that he had taken Hannah out, had cleverly guessed the rest and used it to her own advantage.

Presently Hannah got up. 'Oh, well,' she told the sleeping Paul, 'that's that, isn't it? I can't stop loving him but I must try not to like him any more. And I need not see him…'

She was wrong there. She saw him the very next evening. The van Eysinks had put their heads together and come up with the idea of a surprise farewell party for her. Not a word was said. Henrika arrived and took up her quarters near the nursery and the day was filled with unpacking, discussions about little Paul's routine, his fads and fancies and how to cope with them, and a brief résumé of day-to-day living at the villa. It was almost seven o'clock, with little Paul fed and tucked up and the two girls tidying the nursery between them, when Mevrouw van Eysink came along to see them. Henrika, who was in the secret, grinned as Hannah was told to put on a pretty dress and go downstairs. 'Dinner is later this evening,' explained Mevrouw van Eysink. 'There is a party first, Hannah—for you, so you must hurry up and change and come downstairs. We will have drinks and nice things to eat. Henrika will stay here with Paul and come down to dinner presently.' She beamed at them both and caught Hannah's arm. 'It is so little a thing—but we wish you to know that we say thank you for all that you have done.'

So Hannah showered and changed into one of her pretty short dresses, then went rather hesitantly downstairs to the drawing room, to find it full of people, most of whom she had met at one time or another during her stay. She was given a drink and passed from one group to another, and all of them had something kind to say to her. Presently Mijnheer van Eysink proposed her health and she stood awkwardly, not knowing where to look while they drank, and when she did glance up it was to see Valentijn standing in the doorway with Nerissa beside him. She looked away at once and was glad when Mevrouw van Eysink's mother bore down upon her and engaged her in conversation. Her English wasn't good and Hannah's Dutch totalled a couple of dozen words, so that she was kept fully occupied, and when she had finally satisfied the good lady that her grandson was in the pink of condition and glanced cautiously round, there was no sign of Valentijn. She heaved a sigh of relief, then gave a gasp of surprise as he spoke from behind her.

'Good evening, Hannah. I hope you're enjoying your party, although it's a sad occasion for the rest of us.'

She turned to look at him, relieved to feel quite calm and detached.

'It's a lovely party, thank you, I'm enjoying it very much.' She added slowly: 'Of course I'm going to miss little Paul. Henrika's here, though, and they get on very well together, she's such a nice person…' Her voice trailed away into uncomfortable silence while all the things he had said about her shrieked their way round her head. She would have to make some excuse so that he didn't feel that he had to stand there talking to her, but she was saved the trouble of doing that by Nerissa, who joined them with an airy: 'Hannah, what a lovely party! Do you not feel honoured?'

Hannah met the mocking blue eyes with her own honest grey ones. 'Yes, I do. You must excuse me, there is that aunt of Mevrouw van Eysink's who asked me about little Paul—she's knitting him something…' She smiled blindly at them both and slipped away, and somehow managed to keep out of their way until the guests went. But she hadn't bargained for Nerissa and Valentijn staying for dinner. About half a dozen guests had been invited and Hannah, returning with Henrika just before they all went into the dining room, found that she had been seated on Mijnheer van Eysink's right hand and her place almost obscured by a lovely bouquet of flowers. 'For you to take home,' he told her kindly. 'They will be put in the cellar to keep cool, so they will remain fresh.' He tapped his knife handle on the table and everyone fell silent. 'Hannah, we thank you before our family for all the help you have given us and your devotion to our son. Here is a very small token of that thanks which we hope you will wear and think of us sometimes.'

Hannah opened the box he had given her while

everyone clapped. There was a watch inside, a gold one on a gold band, a dainty thing and elegant. She put it on at once and thanked him in a shy voice, then she got up and walked to the other end of the table where Mevrouw van Eysink sat and held out her hand. 'Thank you too, Mevrouw van Eysink. I've loved looking after little Paul and you. You were one of the bravest patients I've ever known.'

Mevrouw van Eysink pulled her down and hugged her. 'Oh, Hannah,' she cried, 'I do not know how to thank you, only I wish so much that we may meet again.'

Hannah went back to her place and after that the meal became very festive with the kind of food Hannah was sure she would never eat again and champagne to accompany it. And all the time she managed not to look at Valentijn sitting on the other side of the table, and when quite by accident she caught his eye she looked away again at once, but not before she had seen the look on his face—thoughtful and sad and, funnily enough, calculating.

The next time she looked at him, when they were back in the drawing room, he was talking to Mevrouw van Eysink's mother, his face a bland mask.

It was a relief when she saw that little Paul's feed was almost due and she could quite properly excuse herself. She went from group to group saying goodbye, including Valentijn in one of them without actually speaking to him, then she joined Henrika at the door and went upstairs, telling herself how thankful she was that she wouldn't have to see him again.

CHAPTER SEVEN

THE NEXT TWO DAYS passed so quickly that Hannah had no time to sit and mope. She was to leave early on the morning of the third day, and with everything packed she was sitting in the nursery writing down one or two last-minute reminders for Henrika who had gone down to the village for stamps, when Valentijn, unannounced, walked in.

Hannah went white at the sight of him and got up so suddenly that her charts and notes fell on to the floor. He picked them up and put them back on the table and then stood, looking quizzically at her. 'Frightened of me, Hannah?' he wanted to know.

She found her tongue. 'No, of course not—you startled me. Paul's awake if you want to look him over.' She handed over the charts and notes and stood quietly without moving at all while he read them. When he had finished he said:

'Very nice—it looks as though he's out of the

wood,' and then went on: 'You are one of the few women I know who can keep still, Hannah. So often I am distracted by hair patting, finger nibbling, gentle sighs and coughs and even very soft humming—so distracting!'

'We had a very strict Sister Tutor,' she told him woodenly.

'Yes, what's the matter, Hannah?'

Her voice came out a little shrill. 'Nothing. I'm excited. You know, going home and all that.'

He raised thick eyebrows, but all he said, in an impersonal, brisk voice was: 'Well, supposing we have a look at the little chap.'

Which he did, not hurrying himself, his large, well-shaped hands moving gently over the tiny body. At length he straightened up. 'He's fine. You're quite happy about Henrika?'

Hannah was settling Paul in his cot again. 'Oh, yes, thank you, she's wonderful. She'll be here any minute if you wanted to speak to her.'

'I don't think it's necessary. You might try increasing his feed another twenty c.c.s and see how he takes it. Tell Henrika to let me know if he tolerates it—he has a good deal of weight to gain still, hasn't he?'

Hannah removed her finger from Paul's fierce clutch. 'Yes, but you think he'll be all right?'

'With care, yes.' He strolled over to the window and looked down into the garden below. 'I shall be over in London in a week or ten days, and I should like to take you out to dinner, Hannah.'

She said in a stony voice: 'No—no, thank you all the same—I shall be busy.'

His mouth twitched. 'That sounds like an excuse.'

'Well, it is. I don't want to see you ever again. What's more,' her voice despite her best efforts, rose higher, 'I'm quite sure you don't want to see me.'

He had crossed the room in a couple of strides and caught her hands.

'Hannah, what has happened? Something is wrong—last night too…'

The door was pushed wider and Henrika came bouncing in. Valentijn muttered a harsh word which she didn't hear and which Hannah didn't understand anyway, and dropped her hands, to change instantly into a suave doctor visiting a patient, greeting Henrika affably, then chatting for several minutes in their own language until he turned to Hannah with a pleasant:

'Goodbye, Hannah, and all the best for the future.'

She didn't answer him because her throat was closed with tears.

St Egbert's looked grim, dirty and unwelcoming as Hannah's taxi turned into its forecourt. She had had a good flight back with no delays and now she had the rest of the day before reporting for duty in the morning. She would unpack, she decided, see such of her friends who happened to be off duty and then go and see her mother, something she was reluctant to do, because the last two or three letters from home had sounded faintly dissatisfied; moreover, her mother had hinted at a splendid idea she wanted to discuss with Hannah.

Unpacking didn't take long. She shared a pot of tea and a tin of biscuits with several close friends while she answered endless questions about her stay in Holland, caught up on the latest hospital gossip and went, reluctantly, to catch a bus for home.

Number thirty-six looked dingier than ever, colour-less and lifeless under a summer sky which was rapidly being obscured by wispy clouds. And there wasn't much sky to be seen, thought Hannah, longing for the wide skies of Holland, and the trees and quiet lanes and, more than all those, the lovely old house where Valentijn lived.

She opened the flat door with her key and went in, calling to her mother as she did so, and was rewarded by a plaintive: 'So there you are at last, Hannah—I thought your plane got in before lunch.'

Hannah cast her jacket on to the hallstand and went into the sitting room. Her mother was reclining, as she so often did, on the sofa, an open book in her hand. She didn't get up but said: 'I hope you've had lunch, darling, and tea. Dear Mrs Slocombe made me a deli-cious omelette and she always leaves me sandwiches for tea—such a blessing she's been to me!'

She sat up and studied Hannah. 'You're beautifully tanned, but you look…' she paused and gave a little laugh, 'well—plain. I should have thought that after all that luxury you would have been on top of the world.'

'I worked, too, Mother,' said Hannah, and bent to kiss a well made up cheek.

'Yes, dear, I know, but don't bore me with the details—after all, it was only one baby, and at St Egbert's you often get half a dozen, don't you?' Mrs Lang tossed her book on one side. 'It's been so hot in London—you were fine in the country, and with a swimming pool too—I simply can't endure another summer here.'

Hannah sat down. 'You'd like to move, Mother? Why not? I could get a Sister's post in one of the provincial hospitals and we could find a small place…'

She was interrupted. 'I don't mean that at all. I've a much better idea; I'm surprised you hadn't thought of it for yourself. You can leave St Egbert's and work from an agency. I was talking to Mrs Angell at the bridge club and she tells me that an agency nurse can earn a hundred pounds a week on private cases—and think of all the perks and presents! Of course, we couldn't move into a better place at once, but I would be able to have a weekend by the sea now and then, and Mrs Slocombe could stay on.' Mrs Lang darted a glance at Hannah. 'In fact, I've already asked her to.'

'Mother!' Hannah was aghast. 'We can't afford to pay

her—it's forty pounds a week, isn't it?' She made a swift mental review of her money. 'I simply haven't got the money to pay her, and even if you used your pension…'

'Of course I can't do that, heaven knows I pinch and scrape as it is.' Mrs Lang allowed a tear to trickle down her cheek. 'I don't know what I'm going to do. If your father was alive he'd never forgive you for being so uncaring. When he was alive he saw to it that I had the little pleasures of life, and daughters are supposed to look after their mothers—it isn't as if you'll marry…'

Hannah was silent for a few moments, choking back temper and impatience and a whole pile of unfilial feelings. She wanted to shout at her mother that there was no reason why she shouldn't get herself a part-time job and contribute towards the household; move to a country town and do bed and breakfast while Hannah worked at the local hospital, cut down on her spending or just stop moaning about her lot. But she was her mother, she told herself, and she must look after her, and since Mrs Lang enjoyed excellent health then she would have to make up her mind to do just that. It was quite true that she would in all probability never marry—indeed, she would love Valentijn for the rest of her life, and she had never been a girl to put up with second best. And it didn't really matter what she did now, did it? A change might help her to forget.

She said quietly, 'Don't cry, Mother. I'll go and see the Principal Nursing Officer in the morning and resign. I'll have to work about a month still, that will give me time to go round the agencies and choose one.'

'And we can keep Mrs Slocombe?'

'Yes, Mother.' She had been saving for a new winter coat and new boots, she supposed she could manage for another year with her old ones and use the money to pay Mrs Slocombe. She had spent very little money in Holland and she had a pay cheque waiting for her at the office. She got up and put on her jacket. 'Mother, would you help towards Mrs Slocombe's money? Even a few pounds…'

Mrs Lang's tears, which had disappeared immediately she had got her own way, reappeared as if by magic. 'How can I possibly spare a penny? I haven't a thing to wear and everyone else at the bridge club has something new at least each month—heaven knows I'm not extravagant.'

It wasn't worth it, Hannah thought despondently. She had no fight left in her, because she really didn't much care about the future anyway. She would miss the babies dreadfully, but perhaps later on she would be able to go back into hospital. 'I must go, Mother. I'm on duty in the morning. I don't know when I shall be off, but I'll give you a ring, probably in the evening.'

Her mother was smiling again. 'Yes, dear. I'm glad you had such a lovely time in Holland—you modern girls don't realise what wonderful opportunities you get. Did they give you anything?'

Hannah kissed a cheek once more. 'Yes-a watch.'

'You've got one already.' Mrs Lang looked thoughtful. 'Perhaps you could sell it—the money…'

'No, Mother.'

It was something she would keep for the rest of her life, Hannah told herself on the bus going back to the hospital, just to remind her of all the people she had met in Holland. She really meant Valentijn, but she had promised herself that she would forget him. It was going to be difficult; he seemed to be permanently lodged in the back of her head, ready to pop out in an unguarded moment. Sorrow fades and becomes manageable; she knew that after the death of her father, it was just a question of getting through the days until that happened.

Of course the Principal Nursing Officer didn't see eye to eye with Hannah about leaving. 'You have been short-listed for a Sister's post, Staff Nurse,' she pointed out, and it wasn't until Hannah explained carefully, something she hadn't wanted to do, that she conceded to her request.

'I consider it a great waste of a good nurse,' she declared forthrightly. 'Half the time you'll be wasting your talents on patients who could quite well go to their doctor and get pills for their aches and pains. You may occasionally come across a worthwhile case, of course.' She smiled at Hannah. 'I shall be sorry to see you go, Staff Nurse, but I can see you feel it's your duty to leave.' She cast her eye on the calendar on her desk.

'You have five days' holiday due to you, so if you add your two free days for the last week to those, you may leave in three weeks' time.'

So that was that. Hannah broke the news to her friends that evening over their usual pot of tea and after a while gave up trying to explain just way she had to leave.

'You'll hate it! They'll be rich miserable people who treat you like a slave.'

'Yes, I know,' said Hannah unhappily. 'But you see, it's the money.' She got to her feet. 'I promised to telephone Mother, too.'

'There's something else,' declared Pat Rogers, her closest friend, to the room at large. 'She's—well, more unhappy than she should be, and it's as if she can't be bothered…'

'Did she say anything about her job in Holland? I mean, did she meet anyone?'

'I expect she met heaps of people,' declared Louise. She brightened suddenly: 'I say, I wonder if she saw that gorgeous man—what was his name? Uncle Valentijn? I know she didn't like him, but he really was something…' She was about to enlarge upon his attractions when Hannah came back.

Hannah smiled round as she sat down on the bed once more. 'Well, Mother's pleased,' she said.

Three weeks could go very fast when one didn't want them to. Hannah, busier than ever with the prem.

babies, wished every day could be twice as long and when she was off duty went unwillingly from one agency to the next so that she might pick the best one. She had had letters from the van Eysinks and she had written back, bright cheerful letters which didn't mention her change of job. Presently they would stop writing—a card at Christmas, perhaps, for a year or two and then nothing, so there was no need for them to know. And she went home, to listen to her mother's exultant chatter about the things she was going to do with the extra money. Over and above all these, she thought about Valentijn.

It had been no good trying to forget him, not yet at any rate. In bed at night she allowed herself the luxury of remembering each occasion when they had been together. They didn't amount to much, but she relived them constantly, hoping each time she had a letter from Mevrouw van Eysink or Henrika that there would be mention of Uncle Valentijn, but there never was.

He had been coming to England, he had told her, and although she had told him that she never wanted to see him again, she had hoped that he might come to St Egbert's, but he really had no reason to do so, and if Nerissa was with him, as she surely must be, then he wouldn't have the time.

The last day came, and Hannah packed and said goodbye and gave a little party in her room with a bottle of Marks and Spencer sherry and potato crisps and pots and pots of strong tea, and her friends gave her a gift token. Leaving wasn't as bad as she had expected. She had minded far more when she had left the villa; for one thing, she still missed little Paul; none of the babies she had been looking after came anywhere near him, perhaps because they had never been in such danger of their lives as he had been.

She had a job to go to, too, an old lady with pneumonia—she lived in Mayfair and, in return for a ten-hour day, was prepared to pay Hannah a fabulous salary, pay her fares, her laundry and give her meals. The agency lady seemed to think that the job might last two weeks at least and Hannah concluded that the old lady must be very ill; even with antibiotics the elderly sometimes found difficulty in making a rapid recovery. Hannah went home, unpacked, got supper for herself and a jubilant parent, and went to bed, to lie there, imagining Valentijn dancing into the small hours with his glamorous Nerissa.

He was, in fact, sitting in his room at Claridges, thinking about her. He had already discovered that she had left St Egbert's and he had counted on seeing her that evening before he left London for Birmingham, where he was to lecture, and he was annoyed that his plan had come to nothing. It would have to be tomorrow morning. Hannah would surely be at home then, and he could catch a later train. He had messages from the van Eysinks and Henrika, and a report on little

Paul. They could all be dealt with in few minutes, what he really wanted to find out was why Hannah never wanted to see him again. He wasn't a conceited man, but he had thought her initial dislike of him had left her, that she was even beginning to like him as a friend. She grew on one, he reflected, and strangely, she had fitted into his house, like a hand fitting a glove.

The telephone rang and he lifted the receiver and listened to Nerissa's fluting voice asking how he was. He answered briefly, still thinking about Hannah, and on the plea of tiredness, rang off.

Nerissa, at the other end of the line, nibbled at a beautifully manicured finger and frowned. To the best of her knowledge, Valentijn had never been tired in his life.

Hannah saw him the next morning as she was getting off the bus in Brook Street. He had just hailed a taxi and saw her at the same time. She didn't stop to think but dived into Carlos Place and so into the network of narrow streets where her patient lived. She was breathing rather hard as she plied the knocker of the elegant Georgian house, peering over her shoulder, fearful that Valentijn had followed her. As the door was opened she felt disappointment that he hadn't and overwhelming relief at the same time.

The old lady wasn't really ill at all. From the notes left ready for Hannah to read, she had had a small spot of pneumonia on one lung and that had responded to antibiotics. Now she lay in bed, in a pure silk nightie trimmed with real lace, making up her face. She wasn't all that old either. Hannah, who hated shams, was sorely tempted to walk straight out of the house again, but she needed the money very badly. There was Mrs Slocombe to pay and the telephone bill, and she had had to buy uniform dresses and caps…

She spent an hour carrying things to and fro from the bed to the dressing table and back again, and was thankful when the doctor came.

He was nice, very bland too, with a lovely bedside manner, and when she heard his name Hannah knew about him. He gave his services free at at least two children's hospitals and if he thought a patient couldn't afford his fees waived them in the nicest possible way. She warmed to him at once and became very professional while he examined his patient because she sensed that it was expected of her by them. The examination took some time, being interrupted as it was by the lady's complaints about this and that, dealt with smoothly by the doctor and Hannah's willing co-operation. Finally he said: 'Well, dear lady, I think you might sit out for a little while. Nurse Lang will know just what to do to make you comfortable and if there are any ill effects she will report to me at once.'

'How much longer will I have to suffer this dreadful illness?' demanded his patient.

Hannah wondered how he kept a straight face—and yet in a way, the poor woman was ill—ill from having too much of everything and not having to do anything for herself.

'Another ten days, I would imagine, and then I suggest that you take a few days' holiday somewhere quiet—a good hotel perhaps by the sea.'

In the morning room downstairs, taking his instructions, Hannah asked: 'Does Mrs de Courcy really need me here for ten days, sir?'

His eyes twinkled. 'A change from hospital, isn't it, Nurse? I think we can say that length of time. They're not all like this, you know, sometimes one gets a patient who needs nursing. Good day to you.'

Her next case was a charming old gentleman in a Bloomsbury flat who died within four days and her third case was in Mayfair again, a youngish woman, who had had a gastric ulcer and refused to keep to her diet. It was unnecessary for her to have a nurse, but she insisted upon it, declaring that she would die unless she had constant attention, and she had so far driven a succession of young woman almost out of their minds so that their comings and goings had become a kind of routine with the agency staff. Hannah received the suggestion that she might like to try her hand with a passive acceptance with which she accepted everything just lately.

'Let me know when you can't stand it any longer,' the agency lady told her, 'and I'll replace you.'

So Hannah presented herself at the narrow Regency

house in a smart little street in Mayfair and had been admitted by a toffee-nosed manservant who obviously didn't think much of nurses, and led upstairs to her patient, a still pretty woman with a bad-tempered mouth, who greeted her with: 'Oh, you're the new nurse, are you? Well, I hope you understand my case. Doctor Sims will be here shortly. I'll have my bath now and you can help me.'

The day was interminable. It seemed that six o'clock would never come, and when it did Hannah was tired and fed up. Maybe she did earn a good deal of money, but it was no life for her and no job satisfaction. I'll give it a month, she promised herself, strap-hanging on the homegoing bus, and then unless I get a really good case, I'll go back to hospital. Mrs Slocombe will have to go and we'll manage somehow. She couldn't think how at the moment, but anything was better than her present existence.

She tried to explain this to her mother that evening, but it was no use. Mrs Lang merely declared that the next case would be sure to be interesting, and think of the lovely presents Hannah would get. 'You had that perfume from your first case, and the old man's family gave you a gift token...'

Hannah gave up.

She went to work the next morning feeling jaded. Instead of going to sleep she had lain awake thinking about Valentijn. Why had he been in London, and so early in the morning? She had known that he would be coming and at the back of her mind she supposed miserably that she had hoped that he would find her, but he hadn't even tried; after all, he knew where she lived.

Her patient was in a tiresome mood. The diet was killing her, she hadn't slept, she was dying slowly and no one cared. That she had a doting husband, a vague figure in the background Hannah hadn't seen and wasn't likely to, and countless friends who telephoned every minute of the day, were facts she forgot. She took out her ill humour on Hannah, who only half heard it anyway.

They were half way through the morning and having settled her patient comfortably for an hour or so, Hannah had been dispatched to wash the delicate lingerie considered too good for even the best laundry. Hannah was well aware that it wasn't part of her job, especially in a household as well staffed as this one was, but she said nothing; she needed the money, and as her mother had pointed out to her tearfully, beggars can't be choosers.

When the maid came to tell her that she was to go immediately to her patient, Hannah rinsed her hands, dried them and went downstairs to the drawing room, where the lady of the house was reclining in a chaise-longue, trying to remember if she had forgotten to do one of the small chores allotted to her. She couldn't think of anything; it would be some fresh idea her patient had thought up for her own comfort. Hannah sighed and opened the door.

Valentijn was there, standing completely at ease, looking exactly as a respected and well-known member of his profession should look. There was a girl with him, sitting uneasily on the edge of a chair. She was in nurse's uniform, and the patient was on the telephone.

'Good morning, Hannah,' said Valentijn, and gave her a small smile. He looked tired, and behind his bland mask she guessed that he was worried. Nobody else spoke, so she listened to the one-sided conversation being carried on by her patient. Apparently it was with the nursing agency and from the looks she was receiving, it concerned her. The receiver was replaced and her patient turned to Valentijn, her usually cross face wreathed in smiles. 'You really are a most inconvenient man,' she chided him laughingly, 'but the agency assures me that your need is much greater than mine, so I shall do you a great favour and let Nurse Lang go.' She glanced across the room at the other girl. 'Nurse—Smith, is it?—seems a nice enough girl.'

Valentijn was at his most urbane. 'I am eternally grateful to you, Mrs Soames, and I quite realise that you need a nurse to look after you, that is why I took it upon myself to call at the agency and arrange for Miss Lang to be replaced without a moment's delay. I can see that you are a kind and considerate person and can fully understand that only she can help my niece.

Miss Lang looked after the baby from birth and understands him as no one else does, other than his mother, and she is too ill to be of any use.'

Hannah found her tongue. 'Is little Paul ill?' she asked.

Just for a moment his bland mask slipped. 'Yes. I have come to take you to Utrecht to look after him, Hannah.'

She nodded. It wasn't the time to ask questions. She bade her patient goodbye, whisked the nurse away with her to give her a brief résumé of her tasks, and presented herself once more in the drawing room, where she watched Valentijn take a beautifully mannered goodbye of Mrs Soames. He didn't say anything as they left the house, but she was ushered into a waiting taxi and as it set off: 'Could you pack a few things in ten minutes or so, Hannah? I'll explain to your mother. There isn't much time.'

She looked ahead of her. 'How ill is little Paul?'

'Gastro-enteritis—about as bad as he can be.'

Hannah forgot her own problems then and put a hand on his arm. 'Oh, Valentijn, I'm sorry—the poor darling! Is he in hospital? And what's happened to Henrika?'

'Both she and Corinna are ill with gastric 'flu.' He turned his head and looked down at her sympathetic face. 'Hannah, you don't mind? Corinna has worked herself into a fine state and insisted on you looking after little Paul.'

'No, of course I don't mind. She knows I'd do anything to help her.'

Hannah stifled regret that it had been Corinna who had wanted her, not Valentijn, and then chided herself for thinking of herself when it was little Paul who mattered.

'Are we going by boat or from Heathrow?' she asked.

'Neither. I flew my own plane over.'

Which somehow made him seem further away than ever.

Valentijn had a way with him when he chose. She could hear him talking to her mother while she flung what she might need for a couple of weeks into a case, and it said much for his charm that her parent, instead of dissolving into tears, was smiling quite happily.

'So I'm to be left alone once again,' she told Hannah, quite untruthfully, 'but Valentijn has so many good reasons for taking you back with him, I could hardly grumble, could I?' She proffered her cheek for Hannah's kiss. 'Let me know how you get on,' she murmured, 'and the dear little baby—such a shame!'

They were in a taxi, heading for Heathrow, before Valentijn spoke. 'You ran away, Hannah, I had intended calling at your home, but you looked…' he paused…'frightened. I went back to Holland without attempting to see you.'

She said quickly: 'I was surprised, and anyway, I couldn't stop. I was on my way to my first case.'

'Why did you leave St Egbert's?'

'Oh, I—I wanted a change. Will you tell me about little Paul?'

'He became ill suddenly two days ago and on the following day Corinna became feverish with all the symptoms of gastric 'flu, and within hours Henrika had the same symptoms. I had little Paul moved to hospital and flew over this morning to get you.' He added impatiently: 'And the devil of time it took me!'

'Supposing I'd refused? After all, I had my patient.'

He gave a crack of laughter and said coolly: 'I knew you wouldn't refuse, Hannah, and don't try to tell me either that the woman was ill or that you are private nursing because you want to.'

'I have no intention of telling you anything,' said Hannah sweetly, 'but it's hardly the time to argue, is it? Would you tell me about little Paul so that no time is wasted when we get there.'

He stared at her for a long moment. 'If I weren't tired and half out of my mind with worry I would wring your neck, Hannah—what is more, I would have the greatest satisfaction in doing so!'

She didn't reply, but it was nice to know that Valentijn was back in form once more. The bleak look he had given her when she had asked if little Paul was ill had cut her to her loving heart; at least he was in command of himself again. He could be as unpleasant as he wished if it made him feel better and took his mind off his little godson.

They were approaching Heathrow and he said abruptly: 'I'll tell you everything I know in the plane.'

The taxi took them away from the main entrance and the departure buildings. Hannah, very vague as to exactly where they were, was bustled through a small building, offered her passport, had her case examined and was bustled out again. There was a small sports plane standing some distance off and Valentijn strode towards it, carrying her case, while she trotted to keep up. 'Why are you parked here?' she asked breathlessly.

'Special arrangement—in extreme urgency things can be arranged. Besides, I know someone.'

'Trust you!' muttered Hannah, and 'I heard that,' observed her companion.

She was bundled without ceremony aboard the aircraft and sat wordless while he strapped her in and started the engine. It was a four-seater and comfortable, and although she wasn't keen on flying, since Valentijn was the pilot, she had no qualms at all.

When they were airborne, he relaxed and said: 'Now listen carefully, Hannah,' and proceeded to tell her in great detail about little Paul.

'He's isolated, of course, and you will be too, Hannah—I've arranged that at the hospital. He's on boiled water, but he's not tolerating that very well. I set up a drip about two o'clock this morning— Hartmann's solution, and I'm giving him neomycin since it's a coliform organism. The onset was rapid, but there's a chance we got on to it in time. It depends largely on the nursing now.'

'I'll do my best, you know that. Are there any other cases?'

'No, thank God.'

Hannah watched the English coast disappear in the distance. Less than two hours ago she was washing Mrs Soames' smalls…life was full of surprises, and what was it someone said about an ill wind? Although it wasn't kind to think of poor little Paul's illness as of benefit to herself.

After a bit she asked: 'When did you last have a sleep?' She added: 'And a meal?'

'Oh, I had an hour before I left this morning and I had some coffee; I'm not hungry and I assure you that I can go quite a time without a night in bed providing I can get a nap now and then.'

'You'll be fit for nothing if you go on like that,' said Hannah severely. 'I quite see that you haven't had much chance of eating or sleeping, but you really must have a meal and a good sleep when we get to the hospital.'

'I never realised what a bossy girl you are, Hannah.'

'Why should you? Our acquaintance is of the slightest outside our work. And I'm not bossy: I'm thinking about little Paul—suppose he gets worse and you're too cross-eyed with sleep to do much about it?'

'Do you always take the consultants you work for to task in this positive fashion, Hannah?' drawled Valentijn.

'No—I've never done it before. I—I forgot you're a consultant.'

'Oh, good,' said Valentijn.

He brought the plane down on an airfield to the east of Bilthoven, only a few miles from Utrecht, and his car was there. They were in it and away after only a few minutes. Valentijn wasn't only a rich man, reflected Hannah, sitting very upright beside him, he had influence in all the right places too. Life if you were born into the right circles could be totally free of complications.

They drove very fast along the short stretch of motorway and only slowed as they entered the city, where they were held up by the heavy traffic, but Valentijn had his iron self-control back again; he showed no sign of impatience, and watching him, Hannah might be forgiven for thinking he was on his leisurely way to some pleasant outing with time in hand.

He made up for it when they reached the hospital. She was shot inside and into a lift and found herself in the children's unit and Sister's office before she could think anything coherent.

Sister smiled and nodded and then addressed herself to Valentijn in Dutch—a report on Paul, Hannah guessed, and waited quietly.

'He's no better,' she was told tersely. 'Will you take over at once?'

'Of course. I'll need a uniform, though.'

Valentijn spoke to Sister, who nodded and said in quite good English for Hannah's benefit: 'But first you will both have coffee.'

It seemed a waste of time, but it wasn't really—they were both tired and a little travel-weary. Hannah stole a look at Valentijn and marvelled at the self-control which could keep him on his feet for so long, and although his face was strained and pale, he looked very much as usual. He turned and smiled at her and she smiled back, her eyes soft and smiling too.

She felt better for the coffee. Ten minutes later she was in borrowed uniform putting on a gown and a cap and mask, ready to go to her patient.

Little Paul had a room at the end of a narrow corridor and her own room was next to it. She was to sleep there, too, and when she went off duty, Sister had told her, she was to use a door at the end of the passage which would take her directly into the main hospital and avoid the rest of the unit. She would have her meals with everyone else, of course, but at all times she must observe the strictest precautions. It was bad enough having the infant Paul at death's door with gastro-enteritis, but for it to spread to the rest of the hospital would be a nightmare disaster.

She had been told to go in when she was ready and she opened the door to find Valentijn, Sister and the nurse she was to relieve standing round the cot in the almost bare little room. She hardly recognised little

Paul, his small pinched face with its sunken eyes was as white as his pillow. He was asleep, but his breathing was rapid and harsh. Hannah stared down at him and then looked sharply at Uncle Valentijn.

'Yes, Hannah—broncho-pneumonia, unless I'm very much mistaken.' He took off his jacket and got into a gown, no longer looking tired. 'Antibiotics, of course, stat, and then I'll examine him.' After a moment he said softly: 'I'm glad you're here, Hannah.'

'Oh, so am I,' said Hannah. She was going to get little Paul well again—oh, she hadn't the skill and experience of a paediatrician, she knew that, but she had the patience to coax fluids into the tiny mouth, drop by drop, to clean the infant after the continuous vomiting and not to lose heart when he appeared to be making no progress at all. He had fought to live when he was born, and again when he had his op, and now he was going to fight again and she would help him, mopping him up, feeding him when he was able, and mopping him up again. She looked across the cot to his godfather and smiled behind her mask. For the moment she had forgotten that there was anyone else there. 'Don't worry, Valentijn, we'll get him better. He's got well before, he will this time too.'

CHAPTER EIGHT

THE INFANT PAUL made heavy weather of it. Hannah, during the first twenty-four hours, almost lost hope, but then she battled on again, spurred on by the round sunken blue eyes which peeped up at her so listlessly. When Valentijn came for the third or fourth time that day, she had Paul in her arms, drip and all. 'He's fighting very hard,' she told him. 'Do tell Mevrouw van Eysink that, won't you?'

'Of course. Hannah, have you had a meal?'

'Yes, thank you.' She'd had sandwiches in her room because she wasn't going to leave little Paul just yet. 'Did you?'

He smiled behind his mask and she saw his eyes crinkle at the corners. 'Yes, I did as you ordered me to, and had a nap.' He bent over the infant. 'What do you think, Hannah?'

'He's going to get better.'

'Bless you, Hannah!' He had gone again.

She had made her own arrangements with Sister and not told Valentijn. She stayed with Paul until almost midnight, when she was relieved. She ate hastily, had a shower and undressed, then went to bed and slept at once until she was roused as she had requested, at four o'clock. When Valentijn appeared in old slacks and a sweater at six o'clock she was sitting, as neat as a new pin, with Paul on her lap.

'He's better, I think,' she told him. 'He's kept down ten c.c.s of boiled water for more than half an hour.'

He bent over the baby, listening to the tiny chest and then checking the charts. 'His chest's no worse. Go on with the ten c.c.s for the next two hours—I'll be back then and if all's well, we'll increase it.' He took off his gown again. 'You were relieved, Hannah?'

'Yes, thank you—I slept marvellously and they brought me some coffee. Everyone's being super. How are Mevrouw van Eysink and Henrika?'

'Henrika's through the worst, I think, but Corinna isn't trying at the moment.'

'Oh, the poor thing—you will tell her that Paul's kept something down, won't you?'

'Yes. His father's coming in this morning. I must go, I've a clinic at eight o'clock and I must change. I'll be in later, if there's anything urgent Sister knows where to get me—and don't hesitate to send for me.'

The day wore on and Valentijn came and went and found Hannah waiting for him each time, still as neat as a new pin, although there were dark circles under her eyes now. But little Paul had kept down all the tiny amounts of boiled water she had given him and although he didn't look much better, he didn't look any worse and she was sure that his chest was clearer, something confirmed during Valentijn's early evening visit.

Paul van Eysink had been too, in the morning and again that afternoon, his nice face as white as his little son's, pathetically eager to hear any scrap of good news that there might be. 'Corinna's feeling better,' he told Hannah. 'She's so relieved that you're here, Hannah—she wants to see him, but of course, she's not well enough yet.'

'No,' said Hannah gently, 'and by the time she is, we'll have little Paul looking quite his old self again.'

'That's what Valentijn said.' And Paul had gone away full of hope.

It was a little after six o'clock and Hannah had just given the baby his allotted drops of water when Valentijn came in. There was a nurse with him, gowned and masked, as well as Sister. He took Hannah's report, examined the infant closely and said something to the Sister, before turning to Hannah.

'He's holding his own nicely. You're going off duty for an hour—and don't argue, Hannah, we want you fighting fit, and you need a change, however brief.' He pulled down his mask and smiled at her. 'Go and change and be at the entrance in fifteen minutes. I'll tell Zuster de Witteveen exactly what she has to do.'

Hannah went reluctantly, for she didn't care to argue when Valentijn used that tone of voice. And why the front entrance in fifteen minutes, and what was she supposed to do when she got there? An hour, he had said; there was a small park quite close by and there was bound to be a snack bar. She could have a brisk walk and then eat something and be back on duty until the night nurse came to relieve her at ten o'clock. Tonight little Paul was better, she would be able to sleep for a few hours, safe in the knowledge that if anything went wrong she could be at the cotside in seconds.

She showered, changed and was down at the entrance in just over ten minutes to find Valentijn lounging at the top of the steps, talking to two housemen. He put out a casual hand as she went past and brought her to a gentle halt. 'Hullo, you've been quick. Meet two of my housemen—Dirk Wouters and Karel Wintermann.'

He barely gave her time to shake hands before walking her down the steps and into the Bristol.

'Look,' said Hannah, so happy she could have burst but determined to be sensible about it, 'I'm going for a walk in the park and then eat…'

'Oh, dear—did I forget to tell you? You're coming home with me. My housekeeper has a meal waiting and she'll be very hurt if we don't turn up—besides, there's someone I want you to meet.'

'Who?'

'Wait and see.' He was weaving the car in and out of the traffic and then left the busy streets behind to turn into the narrow streets Hannah remembered from the last time, and finally drew up before his home.

As they entered Wilrik came to meet them, according his master a slight bowing of the head and a welcoming smile for Hannah, before opening the double doors of the drawing room for them. Valentijn said something to him as they passed him and then propelled Hannah gently before him into the room. There was someone there, sitting in a chair with a padded back, a small old lady with white hair beautifully dressed and a pair of startlingly blue eyes. She was wearing a black crêpe dress with an old-fashioned high collar and her still beautiful hands were loaded with rings.

'My aunt,' said Valentijn. 'She wanted to meet you.'

Hannah advanced to the chair and offered a hand. The old lady, despite her smallness, looked someone to be reckoned with and Hannah's smile was a little uncertain.

'How d'you do?' observed the old lady. 'So you're Hannah. I've heard about you, of course—you aren't a beauty, but that's not important. Nice figure—nice eyes. I don't hold with these flat women and I've told Valentijn so. I understand you've not much time. Pity, but we'll make the most of what time there is.' She looked across at her nephew, who was standing before the great fireplace, smiling faintly. 'I'll have a glass of sherry and so will Hannah.' She added: 'You've not said a word.'

'Dear Aunt, I lacked the opportunity.' He grinned at her. 'Hannah, sit down and stop looking at the clock, I promise you I'll have you back at the hour.' He got their drinks and came and sat down too, his own drink in his hand, and still with a look of amusement, listened while the old lady questioned Hannah briskly. It was amazing the number of questions which she managed to ask within the next minute or two. Hannah answered them all readily but briefly. Old ladies were notoriously curious about other people, and she rather liked this one. She supplied her age, gave details of her home and childhood, skated delicately over- her mother's idle way of living since her father's death, pronounced herself quite satisfied with her work and agreed that the van Eysinks were a delightful couple and little Paul a remarkable infant. When the old lady snapped: 'And Valentijn what do you think of him?' Hannah refused to be hustled into the wrong answer. She said composedly: 'If anyone can get little Paul better, it will be his godfather.'

She heard Valentijn make a sound which could have been a chuckle, but she didn't look to see. It was her interrogator who observed: 'Discreet, as well.'

She nodded her elderly head and handed Valentijn her glass. 'Well, I'm ready when you are, my dears.'

They dined in a small room Hannah hadn't seen

before, at a round table beautifully set with silver and crystal, and the delicious food was served with no delay at all, so that there was still ten minutes left by the time coffee was brought in.

Valentijn saw Hannah's eyes stray to the grandfather clock against one panelled wall and said soothingly: 'Don't get worked up, Hannah—three minutes to drink your coffee, five minutes to get you back, and two minutes to get to the unit from the car.'

And he was right; there were exactly two minutes left as she got out of the Bristol and when she began a rather hurried thank-you speech, he stopped her. 'I'm coming too,' he remarked, and whisked her into a lift without another word.

The unit was all quietness, broken only by the twitterings and little cries of very small babies. The door at the end of the corridor was shut. Before Valentijn opened it, he bent swiftly and kissed Hannah hard.

She changed in a dream, put on her gown and mask and joined the others by the cot. The nurse nodded at her and Valentijn, gowned and masked now, glanced at her briefly, nothing in his calm impersonal manner betraying the fact that he had been kissing her only minutes earlier.

'We will keep the drip up for another twenty-four hours,' he told her, 'and increase the fluids, starting with the next feed. I'll be in early tomorrow morning, if he's tolerating that we'll get him started on diluted milk.'

His look was as impersonal as his voice, so was his careless nod as he went.

Hannah was too occupied with the infant's needs to have time to indulge her thoughts, but she promised herself that she would get them sorted out in the peace and quiet of her room, once she had been relieved by the night nurse and was in bed.

A sensible resolution which stood no chance against her need for sleep. She was out like a light the moment her head touched the pillow.

She was there, gowned and masked, when Valentijn came early in the morning. The night nurse had gone and little Paul, looking decidedly the worse for wear but much more alive, was awake.

'He's better,' pronounced Valentijn. 'We just have to hang on to him for another forty-eight hours… Let's try him with the diluted milk.' He wrote on the chart and laid it on the desk.

'When are you free today, Hannah?'

'I don't know, but I'm perfectly all right as I am, I can make up for it when he's better.'

'You will be able to get away for a couple of hours this afternoon, I should think—I'll see Sister.'

'Thank you, but if he sicks up after the milk mixture I won't go.'

He raised his eyebrows. 'You'll do as I ask, Hannah, but I don't think he will. I think he's turned the corner.' He added cautiously: 'I'm not committing myself, mind.'

'Why are doctors so—so careful?' she flung at him crossly. 'Of course he's going to get better!'

'Probably because we haven't got your faith.'

Hannah muttered 'Oh, pooh!' as he went out of the door.

He came back again during the morning and when mid-afternoon he came again, he brought the same nurse who had relieved her before. He said with a placid authority she couldn't ignore: 'Go off duty now, please, Hannah, and be back in two hours' time.'

She decided what to do as she changed. The park first because she longed for exercise and fresh air and as far as she could tell from looking out of the window, it was a lovely day; summer was coming to an end, but in the nicest possible way. She got into a pleated skirt and blouse and picked up her blazer. She should have brought more clothes with her, but she hadn't been given much time to pack, had she? She did her hair and face in a rather perfunctory fashion and made her way to the entrance. She was crossing the narrow forecourt when the Bristol purred to a halt beside her.

'Jump in,' said Valentijn in his most avuncular voice.

'I'm going for a walk in the park.'

'Another day. Corinna wants to see you and I think it would do her a great deal of good if you were to tell her personally that little Paul is muddling through. There'll be time for a walk, too.'

He smiled at her with such charm that her heart

stopped and then hurried its beat so that she had to swallow it back to its place. 'Very well,' she said, and added idiotically: 'Are you free too?'

He leaned over and opened the door wider and when she had settled herself closed it before driving on. 'I had a teaching round this morning and a small clinic. I see my private patients this evening.'

'Babies—private patients?' asked Hannah in a surprised voice.

'Quite a few—in their own homes, of course. Feeding problems and small malformities which I can correct without having to take them into hospital. Have you heard from your mother, Hannah?'

'Yes, she's fine, Mrs Slocombe goes each day.'

'You will return to your private nursing?' He asked the question idly.

'Well, yes—I'll have to…' She stopped, angry that her tongue had run away with her.

'To pay for Mrs Slocombe?' Valentijn made the suggestion so quietly that she went on quite naturally.

'Yes, she costs an awful lot, you know, and I can earn almost twice as much.'

'But you prefer hospital.'

'Oh, lord, yes—I miss it dreadfully.' She stopped again. She mustn't whine about it, above all to him. 'But I'm sure to get an interesting job when I get back—it's a very good agency.' She turned her head and smiled at him, but he was staring in front of him, his profile stern, so she went on in a flurry: 'How is Nerissa—I mean Juffrouw van der Post? I expect you see a great deal of each other, it must be very nice for you—I mean, to have her to talk to when you're finished at the hospital.'

Valentijn threw her a quick glance and she saw that his eyes were cold and hard; she'd said the wrong thing again, he would tell her any minute to mind her own business.

He didn't. He said in an expressionless voice: 'As a matter of fact I haven't seen her since Paul was taken ill.'

Relieved that she wasn't to have her head bitten off, Hannah ploughed on. 'How silly of me—of course you wouldn't want her to risk getting the 'flu or picking up a bug.'

'I don't seem to have been as thoughtful with you, Hannah.'

'But I'm a nurse.'

He gave a chuckle. 'I tend to forget that. Here's the villa. You'll find Corinna downstairs in the small sitting room. Go on in—I'll be along presently.'

So Hannah went inside, to be met and welcomed and taken to Mevrouw van Eysink who was sitting in a chair looking out of the window, doing nothing.

She looked up as Hannah went in and gave a delighted shriek. 'Hannah! I told Uncle Valentijn I wanted to see you, but I never thought you could be spared. Oh, this is splendid—we'll have tea and you can tell me all about little Paul.' Her lip trembled and a tear trickled down her cheek. 'Oh, Hannah, is he going to be all right? You can't imagine how awful he looked, and we had no idea what to do, and poor Henrika and I, we felt ill too.'

Hannah sat down. 'Little Paul's getting better,' she said positively. 'Uncle Valentijn said so, didn't he, and he wouldn't tell lies about that. Paul's beginning to take his feeds again and he gained just a very little today. Mevrouw van Eysink, you have to get quite well and strong so that you can help Henrika look after him. He's growing all the time, you know, and soon he'll be noticing things and sitting up and playing with his toys—you'll have your hands full. And you? Are you feeling almost well again?'

'Oh, yes, I am, especially now I know that little Paul is getting better. And Henrika telephoned this morning to say that the doctor says she may come back in a week. Will little Paul be better then, do you think?'

'You'd better ask Uncle Valentijn and see what he says.'

'Uncle Valentijn says in all probability he will be.'

Hannah wondered how long he had been standing listening to them as she watched him saunter across the room and bend to kiss his niece. She was rendered speechless when he strolled across to her too and kissed her as well.

'You look very nice, the pair of you, sitting there,' he observed, apparently by way of explanation.

Hannah had gone very red, but she kept her cool with something of an effort. 'I'm glad to see Mevrouw van Eysink looking better than I expected,' she remarked in a no-nonsense voice. "Flu makes you feel rotten.'

'Indeed it does.' He spoke gravely, but she knew he was laughing at her. 'Corinna, I promised Hannah a walk, shall we have tea first or afterwards?'

'Now,' said his niece promptly, 'and may I come too?'

Hannah's, 'Oh, please do,' was so prompt that Valentijn laughed out loud.

They strolled round the gardens, with Corinna well wrapped up because the late afternoons were beginning to get a little chilly. She walked between them, chattering away quite happily, making plans for little Paul's return and declaring that she felt almost well again and when could she see him.

'Oh, a few days yet,' declared Valentijn easily. 'He's on the mend, but Hannah will have to put in quite a lot of work on him—let's say in four days' time—and don't expect a bouncing baby, *liefje.*'

'Oh, any kind of baby,' cried Corinna.

They didn't talk much as they drove back to the hospital. When they were almost there, Hannah thanked her companion in her gentle voice and nipped smartly away. Back on duty again it seemed to her that the pleasant little interlude had never been, although

there were memories to prove that it had—Valentijn's
kiss, for example. Perhaps, she allowed herself to hope,
he would take her out the next day as well.

But although he came three times, he was nothing
if not impersonal in his manner. Only as he was leaving
he interrupted a conversation with Sister to switch to
English and address Hannah.

'You will take two hours off between six o'clock and
eight o'clock, will you? Zuster can't get a nurse to
relieve you before then.' He added formally: 'I'm sorry.'

When Zuster Witteveen arrived, Hannah changed
quickly and went down to the entrance. There was no
one there waiting for her, and she hadn't really
expected it. She had had two lovely outings with
Valentijn and really there had been no need for him to
bother with her. She walked briskly through the park
and out of its further gate, had coffee and a sandwich
at a little snack bar and started back through the streets.
She was waiting at a crossing when she saw the Bristol
with Valentijn at the wheel and Nerissa beside him. She
was talking animatedly, but he was looking straight
ahead, but with all that traffic around he had no choice.
Hannah stared after him for as long as the car remained
in sight, then nipped across at the tail end of the
crossing and earned a frown from a passing policeman.

She hurried back, trying not to think of the two
people in the car. They would be on their way to dine
and dance, she supposed; Nerissa would be a delight-

ful companion for an evening out; beautiful to look at
and entertaining too. Hannah ground her small white
teeth, hating her. It was somehow comforting to get
back to the haven of the hospital room and sit with little
Paul on her knee, watching his valiant efforts to finish
his minute feed.

She saw Valentijn the following morning, and when
Sister said that she could be relieved for three hours
that afternoon she resolved to refuse any offer he might
make to take her out, but he made none, so she went
shopping, buying dull things like soap and tissues and
choosing a present for her mother. And in the evening,
when she was back on duty, Valentijn had nothing to
say other than instructions about little Paul.

She was told quite early in the morning that she
could have the same off-duty. The infant was making
headway now, and she thought privately that it
wouldn't be long before her services would no longer
be needed. In another few days Henrika would be back
and presumably the baby would go home then. She
would visit a museum or two; there would be time
enough, and she had enough money to have a cup of
tea or coffee somewhere. The weather was overcast
and she was thankful that she had packed a raincoat.
Dressed in blouse and skirt and heartily sick of both,
she put on the raincoat and went down to the entrance.
She was going through the door when the porter hailed
her and handed her a note. Valentijn's unintelligible

scrawl invited her to wait where she was until he came
and he was hers, V. v. Bertes. She could of course
ignore it, although she didn't want to, or leave a
message with the porter. It would have to be a written
one, though, and since she had made up her mind not
to go out with him again, she went back to the porter's
lodge, rummaged round in her bag for paper and pen,
and started to write. Half way through her carefully
worded refusal she was aware that Valentijn was
bending down and reading it over her shoulder.

'You went shopping yesterday,' he said mildly, 'you
couldn't possibly want to do so again today.' He
straightened up. 'Besides, Aunt would like you to have
tea with her. She likes you.' He added in a wheedling
fashion: 'She's very old.'

'Well, I—I need the exercise. Perhaps I could walk
there and just stay a little while with her. I like walking.'

'Now that's funny—so do I. There's a pleasant
stroll through the park missing most of the traffic.
We'll go that way.'

'There's no need…' began Hannah, and glanced
fleetingly at his face, to find him smiling in a particularly disarming fashion, so she looked away again.

'None at all,' he agreed airily, 'but it would be an
opportunity to discuss Paul, and then there's the
question of getting him home again, and I daresay you
will want to leave then.'

Hannah's heart sank at the very thought, but she said

in a matter-of-fact voice: 'Well, yes, I should be glad to know what you've decided.'

They went out into the dull afternoon together and she wished she had something else to wear other than the elderly raincoat, especially as her companion had a gaberdine car coat which, even when donned with a complete disregard for his appearance, managed to look what it was, a very expensive garment which fitted perfectly.

The park was nice, bright with dahlias and early chrysanthemums and ornamental trees and shrubs; the grass was smooth and green and in one corner there were children on a line of swings. There were dogs too and Hannah, for something to say, asked: 'Have you a dog?'

'Yes—a bull mastiff—Nipper. We take each other for a walk every morning before work and again in the evening, the rest of the day he spends in the garden or with Wilrik, unless I'm home, of course.'

'I like dogs,' said Hannah. 'Father had a retriever, but when he died and we moved to London we gave him to friends. I—I missed him.'

'They're good company. Paul and Corinna are going to get a puppy to grow up with little Paul.'

'He'll do now, won't he?' Hannah had forgotten that she hadn't meant to see any more of Valentijn; he was splendid company and she felt quite at ease with him; she had even forgotten Nerissa.

'I think and hope so. He's taken an awful beating,

poor little chap, but he's tough. He's gained again too. I think we might let him go home in another three days. Henrika can settle in a day before that, and if you would stay for a couple of days just to see that everything is running smoothly, and I know Corinna wants you to have at least one day as their guest before you go. Don't worry about your flight; I'll see to it when we know exactly when you're going. Are you all right for money?'

Hannah had almost nothing in her purse, but she wasn't going to say so. She told him that yes, she had enough to tide her over until she returned home. She had spent very little and there was the cheering prospect of her salary waiting for her at the agency when she got back. She would have to get another case at once, though.

As though he read her thoughts, Valentijn asked: 'Have you a case to go to?'

'Not exactly,' said Hannah, and thought what a silly reply that was.

But he didn't pursue the subject, talking about this and that; and never saying a word about Nerissa.

Arrived at his front door, Wilrik, who must have been lying in wait, opened it with a flourish, bestowed a benevolent smile upon Hannah, and took their coats before preceding them across the hall to open the drawing room doors. He bent a dignified ear to what Valentijn had to say to him and melted away to the kitchen quarters.

There he sat himself down in the armchair, reserved
solely for his own use, removed a newspaper from his
inside coat pocket and spread it out, but before reading
it he observed to his wife, busy with the tea tray: 'She's
here again, and as nice a young lady as I ever did see.
Very *deftig* she is too, just right for the master. That
other one's no good for him.'

'You're right there,' observed his wife. 'But don't
count your chickens, Wilrik. Do they speak English
together?'

'Always. She doesn't speak our language, not yet,
but she'll learn quick enough—such a nice young
lady.' Wilrik sighed and picked up his paper.

'She'll not have much chance against the other
one…'

'Her eyes are grey. Very soft and gentle they are too.'

Hannah, happily unaware of this conversation,
greeted Valentijn's aunt, took the chair indicated to her
and listened happily enough to the old lady's flow of
talk. She rambled a little from time to time and once
or twice nodded off into a light doze, to awake re-
freshed after a few minutes and go on again, describ-
ing various members of the family, the houses they
lived in and their various children, 'And it's about time
you started a family, Valentijn,' she remarked suddenly.
'This great house—and you rattling round it like a
pea in a pod.'

Her nephew stretched out in a great armchair close

to her, grinned and said meekly that he'd think about it, and would she like her tea?

It was served by Wilrik, looking more dignified than ever, and presently when they went to the french windows in order to walk in the garden, he was there again to open them, smiling in a fatherly fashion at Hannah.

The garden was lovely, much bigger than Hannah had expected. She admired the flowers and the shrubs at some length and then asked: 'Do tell me, does Wilrik always open all the doors for you? I mean, he seems to pop up…'

Valentijn laughed. 'I suspect he is interested in you. Usually I am permitted to open doors for myself. We are good friends, he and I; he has been with the family for almost all his life. It has been suggested that he should retire, but I will not hear of it; he stays until he wants to go, and I think that will be never.'

'He's nice,' said Hannah. The suggestion would have come from Nerissa, of course. She would want someone young and smart in a striped waistcoat to answer her door. Her door—it didn't bear thinking about.

They went back inside presently and bade the old lady goodbye, then were ushered into the street once more, and this time Hannah smiled warmly at Wilrik. He was part of the house, and that was part of Valentijn and therefore to be loved.

Little Paul was making rapid progress at last and he

was to go home in two days' time. Valentijn had said so when he came the next morning. 'Henrika will go to the villa tomorrow,' he told Hannah in a pleasantly impersonal voice, 'and have everything ready for you both, and if you would like to arrange to leave two days from then,' just for a moment his voice wasn't impersonal at all, 'Corinna wished me to tell you that they would like you to stay for longer than that if you could do so—a week, perhaps.'

If she was never going to see him again, she might as well get it over with. 'I have to go back,' she said steadily. 'It's very kind of the van Eysinks to invite me, but I—there's sure to be a case waiting,' she finished rather lamely.

She spent her free time alone that day, and the day following too, and when Valentijn came to the ward, he was coolly friendly and didn't even ask her what she had done with her off duty, or indeed, if she had had any!

On her last day she was free after her dinner. She packed her few things ready for an early start in the morning, and decided to go for a walk. There was still plenty of time for her to see…

She was on her way through the hospital when she met Valentijn, coming up the stairs two at a time. 'Ah, there you are,' he exclaimed genially. 'I got held up. Aunt is expecting you.'

Hannah stood poised, giving, she hoped, the impression that she was on her way to somewhere important and immediate. 'Oh, I didn't know—I'm just on my way to—to the shops, something I forgot, and I'm on duty again in an hour, just over an hour.'

'One hour and twenty minutes, to be exact. We can stop at whichever shop you want on the way.' He smiled at her, his eyes half shut. 'Besides, I want to talk to you—your ticket home and one thing and another— I told Corinna I'd see to it. Paul's away for a couple of days on business.'

Hannah started to walk down the steps behind him. She had done her best; and her heart, delighted at the prospect of a short time in his company, had completely overruled her head.

The Bristol was outside, but before Valentijn opened the door he asked: 'Would you rather walk, Hannah?'

Walking would do her more good, but on the other hand she might never get the chance to ride in a Bristol motor car again. She told him so and although he only smiled and held the door open, she missed the sudden gleam in his eyes. Half way to the house she reminded him: 'You wanted to tell me something about my ticket.'

'Ah, yes, there's nothing available until Friday, I'm afraid—that's a day later than you wanted, isn't it? Let me see, it's Monday today, you both go to the villa tomorrow, that leaves you Wednesday to settle in with Henrika and a day over—Corinna will be delighted. She feels bad about your lack of free time since you've been over here. It's a morning flight, by the way.' He glanced at her sideways. 'I'm going to Brussels for a couple of days.'

Hannah forgot about her own plans and fastened on the only thing that mattered. 'Oh, are you? When?'

'Late tomorrow night—I'll drive down.'

'You won't be back before I leave,' and when he didn't answer she plunged into a string of banal remarks about little Paul, none of which merited a reply, until they reached his house.

Wilrik forgot his dignity entirely and beamed at her, hurrying to open the doors and murmur to Valentijn. 'Tea,' Valentijn told her. 'Wilrik says there's English cake for tea in your honour.'

'How very kind—what a dear he is!' Hannah frowned, standing in front of the half open drawing room door. 'Now, if only I could speak Dutch—but I only know a dozen words, just enough to get me through the day at the hospital. None of them seem right for thanking someone for cake for tea.'

Valentijn gave a crack of laughter. 'Never mind, I'm going to tell Wilrik what you say: he'll love it.'

Wilrik did. His severe features broke into a smile and he bowed his head and then said something to Valentijn very softly. Valentijn's features all at once assumed their bland expression and Hannah, knowing every line and wrinkle of his face by now, guessed he was angry about something.

'Did I say something?' she asked. 'Have I annoyed you—both of you, perhaps?'

The bland look melted. 'Certainly not—Wilrik is very pleased.' He spoke to the elderly man then and gave Hannah a gentle prod. 'Aunt is waiting, there'll be tea and that cake in a moment.'

They stayed with the old lady for half an hour and with Nipper's enthusiastic co-operation, disposed of the cake, and when Hannah bade the old lady goodbye, she was invited to kiss the delicately tinted cheek. 'No need to say goodbye,' said Valentijn's aunt, a remark Hannah put down to her being so elderly that she tended to forget things.

At the hospital she wished Valentijn goodbye as well, 'Because I don't suppose I'll see you before we go,' she pointed out a little too brightly.

'Probably not, but I may come out to the villa during the day just to look little Paul over.' He smiled down at her, his eyes twinkling. 'How proper of you, Hannah, to choose somewhere to say goodbye where I can't do more than shake your hand. I'll have to make sure of that visit tomorrow, won't I?'

There was nothing more to say to that. Hannah muttered something silly about being late and rushed inside. It would be wonderful to see him again, but would she be able to bear it, she wondered, it would only prolong the agony?

CHAPTER NINE

THE RETURN to the villa was made soon after nine o'clock in the morning with baby Paul, fast asleep after his feed, on Hannah's lap on the back seat while Mijnheer van Eysink drove the Mercedes.

Their departure had been something of an event, with Sister and the housemen to see them off and a chorus of good wishes to send them on their way. Mijnheer van Eysink drove slowly as though he were afraid that any speed above forty miles an hour would harm his very small son, and as they neared the villa he said over his shoulder, 'I've told everyone to stay away for a few more days, Hannah. He mustn't be upset in any way. He still looks very small…'

'He is very small,' observed Hannah matter-of-factly, 'but I promise you now he's got over this, he'll make strides—it's just a question of putting on weight, and he's gaining every day now, and remember he's older and that much stronger.'

'Valentijn said that, too. We're sorry you can't stay, Hannah. Perhaps you would like to come and spend a week with us in the spring? It's very pretty then.'

'I should like that very much, although I expect I'll have to fit in my holidays when and where I can.' Or no holidays at all, she added silently, because while she was on holiday she would earn nothing.

It was nice to see Mevrouw van Eysink looking quite fit again and Henrika as large and placid as usual, ready and waiting for them in the nursery. Hannah unpacked, tucked little Paul into his pram and strolled round the garden with Henrika and Mevrouw van Eysink until a sudden darkening of the skies sent them indoors. Little Paul had been fed and settled for his nap and the three of them had had lunch when Mevrouw van Eysink said suddenly: 'Hannah, you shall be free—now, this minute. Here are the two of us to mind little Paul and you have had almost no time to yourself for days. You are to go and enjoy yourself for the rest of the afternoon. Is that not a good idea?'

She looked around her in triumph and Henrika echoed her at once. 'There is nothing to do, Hannah, and it is true you have had not enough fresh air. It is good weather again and you can walk…'

'Or ride?' asked Mevrouw van Eysink.

'Well, I'd love a walk; I've always wanted to find out where all those bridle paths went to—you know, the woods beyond the first village.'

'Oh, they are delightful. You can walk for miles…'

'Yes, but will I know where I am?'

'Of course,' Henrika laughed. 'There are signposts with the names written on them.'

And so there were, Hannah discovered an hour or so later, only unfortunately they meant nothing to her. She had neglected to look at a map before she started out so that now, confronted with a signpost pointing to four different places, she had no idea which to take. She was quite lost. Trees stretched in all directions, intersected by bridle paths and narrow footpaths. If only the sun would come out! It was five o'clock by now and she wanted her tea, she was tired and hot and thirsty and just a little frightened. Common sense told her that if she kept to one path sooner or later it would arrive somewhere, only what to do when the path forked?

She walked on, trying not to notice that the sky was darkening again and that a thin wispy mist was rising among the trees, and presently she came to a small clearing with six paths radiating from it. And now she was scared. A process of elimination, she told herself in too loud a voice, and chanted 'Eeny, meeny, miny, mo' until only one path was left. It was a pity that it was the one nearest and the narrowest and darkest of them all.

She had gone perhaps fifty yards along it when she heard her name, Valentijn, hearteningly enormous and solid, was standing in the clearing. Hannah didn't stop to think but raced back, to fling herself into his arms.

They closed round her in a gentle grip and held her tight, and she buried her face in his shoulder and wailed. 'Valentijn, oh, Valentijn, I was thinking about you and now you're here!' She lifted grey eyes filled with tears to his face and smiled shakily, her feelings so plain that they might have been written in her face.

He didn't speak, only held her close and kissed the top of her head, and when she would have drawn back, he tightened his hold.

'My poor dear, you've been scared out of your wits, haven't you? I'll take you back at once, they're all a bit anxious, but fortunately Henrika remembered that you wanted to explore the woods.'

He held her away from him and looked down into her face. She had never seen him look like that before, tender and kind and more than that; looking at her as though he had discovered something precious. Perhaps if she hadn't seen that look she wouldn't have said what she said now. The words tumbled out and she was unable to stop them, although she knew that she would come to regret them bitterly later.

She stared back into his blue eyes and blurted out: 'Valentijn, there's something… I've been wanting to say it and now I can't stop myself, only you're not to take any notice because you're going to marry Nerissa. I love you—I think I fell in love with you weeks ago, only I didn't know, not at first. And I'm telling you now because it wouldn't be fair to you not to tell you, would it? You might think that I don't like you at all, and that would be dishonest of me, wouldn't it?' She smiled a little shakily. 'I feel better now I've told you.'

'Hannah—little Hannah…!'

His voice was kind and concerned, but she didn't look at him now. She interrupted him quickly, 'Oh, it's quite all right. I hope you and Nerissa are going to be very happy.'

He didn't speak for a moment, then: 'Dear Hannah—we must talk, there are things I have to say, but not now. I'm going to take you back to the villa, and later we'll go somewhere quiet and talk.'

'It's quiet here…'

Valentijn sighed and she felt the warmth of her feelings chill with it. 'Hannah, I have to go out this evening—I'm already late…'

The chill turned to ice, and to cover her confusion and misery she said brightly: 'Oh, how thoughtless of me—let's go at once. I'm keeping you dawdling around…' The regrets she had stifled only a few minutes ago were choking her. Whoever had said that silence was golden had been right; if only she could unsay all the things she had said! Still brightly she asked: 'Whatever would have happened if I'd kept straight on?'

'You would have ended up on an airfield rather a long way from the villa. Hannah, I must talk to you, but there's no time—later this evening I'm driving to

Brussels, you know that, and I don't think I can get away for at least three days—we'll talk then.'

He seemed to have overlooked the fact that she was leaving the day after the next, but it didn't matter, in fact it was a good thing. She murmured something and repeated: 'Shall we go? Am I very far from a road?'

Valentijn didn't seem to mind changing the subject. 'No, about ten minutes' walk—down this bridle path.' He threw an arm round her shoulders and they walked side by side down it until Hannah saw the road and the Bristol parked under the trees. A relief, for the light-hearted chat she had been struggling to maintain as they walked along hadn't been very successful, and Valentijn hadn't helped at all, giving brief answers in an absentminded way. He would be feeling embarrassed, she decided, just as she did, fool that she was, putting him in an intolerable situation and covering herself in shame. She became silent and Valentijn, seeing her unhappy face, began to talk at last, easily and with no sign of awkwardness, and he went on talking as they drove back, giving her an account of an interesting case he had seen that morning, giving her time to pull herself together.

At the villa he went in with her, explained to an anxious Corinna what had happened and as Hannah made for the stairs, called a casual goodbye. She called back over her shoulder without stopping and Valentijn stood watching her until she had disappeared, his eyes very bright, his mouth set in a grim line. And he in turn was watched by Corinna, who instantly begged him to stay for dinner. 'You can drive down to Brussels from here and pick up your things as you go,' she pointed out.

'There's nothing I should like better,' he told her, 'but I can't, my dear. I'll be gone for three days. Try and keep Hannah here until I get back, I want to talk to her.'

He left at once, driving very fast back to Utrecht. He was already late for the date he had with Nerissa.

Hannah didn't go downstairs again for quite some time. In the nursery she declared stoutly that she would see to little Paul, while Henrika had half an hour to herself. 'And I'll do the early morning feed,' she offered. 'I'm sure to wake early and it'll give you a chance to lie in.' So it was an hour or more before she rejoined Mevrouw van Eysink. Mijnheer van Eysink wasn't home yet and the two of them sat companionably chatting while they waited for Henrika to join them.

'You had a nice walk, even though you got lost?' Mevrouw van Eysink wanted to know.

'Oh, yes! It was lovely in the woods—I was a fool not to have looked at a map first.'

'You were glad to see Uncle Valentijn, I expect?' Corinna glanced sideways at Hannah, who wasn't looking. But she did go pink and her companion looked pleased.

'Yes, I was—I—I was getting a bit scared. I feel rather

awful because I didn't thank him—perhaps you would tell him how grateful I was when you see him again?'

'Of course I will.' Mevrouw van Eysink sounded remarkably cheerful, one had the impression that she was going to burst into song at any moment. 'He's gone, as you know, to Brussels. He would not stay for dinner because he had an appointment first.' She gave Hannah a sudden gleeful smile. 'You know, Hannah, I believe he is not going to marry that Nerissa after all. I asked him a few days ago when he and Nerissa were going to fix the wedding day and he laughed and said: "Fix the day? *au contraire*, my dear niece".'

Hannah had gone from pink to white and then pink again. 'Oh, did he say that?' Her smile widened and her eyes sparkled. 'Then that's why…' She remembered all the things which had puzzled her and now were a puzzle no longer. On the other hand, Valentijn had been silent when she had blurted out that she loved him. Perhaps he didn't want to marry anyone, perhaps he had used her as a kind of stopgap while he got over Nerissa. Hannah frowned. It seemed strange to her that even though Nerissa was a girl she detested, any man, and that included Valentijn, wouldn't be proud to show her off as his wife; she was beautiful and always well-groomed and she had a lovely smile, even though, thought Hannah waspishly, it was an entirely false one. And after all, what had she herself to be happy about; Valentijn had taken her out once or twice, taken her to his home, even kissed her, but he could have done any of these things to any girl and meant nothing by them. She needed to know more and she was about to embark on a few careful questions when Henrika and Mijnheer van Eysink appeared simultaneously and the chance had gone.

She slept very little that night, vacillating between hope that Valentijn might love her just a little and despair that she wasn't going to see him again, anyway, so she would never know. She decided, just before she slept at last, that the quicker she went home the better. Mevrouw van Eysink had been most insistent that she should stay another two or three days. Her ticket could be changed, she had said urgently, and the rest would do Hannah good. But Hannah had said firmly that she must get back home and she would prefer to catch the early morning flight as had been arranged for her. She woke to little Paul's grumpy little mutterings and got up to see to him. Her last day, she thought sorrowfully, and could have wept. She would remember it always, she told little Paul as she tucked him cosily back into his cot.

Several hours later she knew that to be true, but not for any happy reason. They had had lunch and Hannah, egged on by her companions, was on the point of going for a last walk. She had refused the loan of the mare; the sky looked threatening and if it rained she would be able to take shelter more easily on her own, so she got into her raincoat and prepared to go out. She was actually going out of the front door when Nerissa drove up in her smart sports car and before Hannah could avoid meeting her, had got out of the car and come to meet her.

'Oh, I'm so glad to find you in!' she exclaimed prettily, and tucked an arm into Hannah's. 'I wanted to see you…I know you'll be pleased…'

'Why?' asked Hannah, very much disliking the arm.

She was being drawn round the side of the villa towards the swimming pool, and no one was sitting on that side of the house, so her chances of rescue were slim. She managed to come to a halt half way down the path, though. 'I'm going for a walk,' she explained. 'I don't suppose it's very important, is it?'

Nerissa looked roguish. 'Oh, it is to me,' she said with sickening archness, 'and anyway, you must have guessed, Hannah—we quarrelled, Valentijn and I— oh, a silly—what do you say in English—lovers' tiff, so I went away for a few days and when he came back, he was…' She broke off with a tinkle of laughter. 'Well, you understand, and so unhappy…' She touched a gold chain with a heart-shaped pendant hanging from it. 'He gave me this, isn't it charming? And so we've fixed the wedding day—and all because of you, Hannah.'

'Why?' asked Hannah for the second time. Her mouth had gone dry and there was a lump of ice somewhere inside her, but somehow she contrived to appear casual.

'He said that taking you out made him realise how

much he missed me—such a compliment to me, don't you think? And last evening…'

Hannah gave herself away completely. 'Oh, is that why he said he had to go…?'

Nerissa's blue eyes narrowed, but she said quickly, 'Yes, yes, of course, we had a date. Didn't he tell you? Although there was no reason why he should, was there? He had to drive like a demon.'

Hannah said in a puzzled voice: 'Yes, but he was going to Brussels.'

'Well, of course, but we spent the evening together at my flat before he left—it's not a long drive.' Nerissa turned and looked at Hannah, and Hannah saw the spite and triumph in the beautiful eyes. 'You're leaving early in the morning, aren't you? Such a pity that you won't see Valentijn again—but perhaps it's just as well.' She gave her little tinkle of laughter again and Hannah went red. So he had told Nerissa. Probably they had laughed about it, although to give Valentijn his due, his laughter would have been kind. She mumbled something and said over-brightly: 'Well, I must go for my walk. I do hope you have a lovely wedding and that you'll both be very happy.' She didn't offer to shake hands. With a smile which almost killed her she uttered a cheerful 'Goodbye,' and made off.

As she marched along the lanes in the direction of the village her cheeks burned like fire. No wonder Valentijn hadn't answered her! She shuddered at the memory, still vivid, of the things she had said. Thank heaven she would never see him again; it might break her heart, but it would save her pride. He had used her as a stopgap until Nerissa returned, to be welcomed with heart-shaped lockets and love. She sniffed forlornly, longing to be back in England where she could forget the whole business. She went through the village, past the little café where she had met Valentijn, and followed the path they had taken together.

It was raining by now, a steady Dutch downpour from skies which had become leaden, weather which suited her mood. Her raincoat, not proof against such an onslaught, was soaking; she could feel water trickling down under its collar and a chilly damp where the rain had soaked through its shoulders. Her feet were wet too, and as for her hair, it had been washed and blown out of its tidy bun on top of her head, and hung in untidy sopping streamers. But the rain didn't matter. She was remembering their ride together along the very path, and presently when she reached a convenient tree stump, she sat down on it. It was lonely there and the afternoon was unnaturally dark because of the weather, but at least she could have a good howl in peace, and there was no need to wipe away her tears; her face was already wet with rain.

When Valentijn said very quietly behind her: 'Hannah?' she nearly fell off the stump with fright, but she didn't turn round, only said gruffly and with a shocking lack of manners: 'What?'

She heard his little laugh and turned her head to look at him. After all, she could have imagined his voice, for her head was full of him.

'Hannah, darling Hannah, I thought you might be here, because this is where we came riding together.'

She took no notice of that, focusing her eyes beyond him so that she didn't have to look at his face she asked: 'Why are you here? You were to go to Brussels—you went—Nerissa said so, she said... she said that you wouldn't be back before I went home.'

He came slowly towards her, his hands thrust into the pockets of his burberry. 'Nerissa said a great many things,' he observed. 'If I had known...' He sighed. 'I should have found time to talk to you, my dearest heart, but little Paul was ill and you were like a mouse down a hole every time I looked for you. And I couldn't tell you yesterday because I hadn't seen Nerissa then and I had to finish with her before I asked you to marry me.'

'Marry me?' Hannah got up from her stump and stood facing him.

'Yes, you, my darling. You see, I thought that if I married Nerissa she might cure my loneliness. I didn't love her, but she was good company and always there—and then I met you and I knew then that if I married her I'd be lonelier than ever and that it was you I wanted for my wife.'

They were close to each other now, although

Hannah didn't look at him but examined his handmade brogues as though her very life depended upon it.

'When you came to my house I wanted you to stay there for always. You're so right, so exactly right; I could see you so clearly in my mind's eye sitting in that little armchair, knitting or whatever, with the light shining on your pretty hair and the children doing their lessons round the table and a baby in its high chair.'

Hannah looked up then. 'That's funny,' she told him. 'That's exactly what I dreamed of too—only I thought it could never happen.'

He pulled her gently close. 'Oh, yes it could, and it will, just as quickly as possible.' He kissed her wet face gently and then with a force which took her breath. 'My dearest darling. I'm so in love with you—I couldn't let you go, I had to come back and talk to you. I asked Corinna to persuade you to stay until my return, but she telephoned me and I came at once. I guessed then that Nerissa had been to see you...'

'Yes, she did come.' Hannah tucked her wet cheek against his shoulder. 'But it doesn't matter what she said now. Do you really want to marry me, Valentijn?'

'More than anything in the world, darling Hannah, and as soon as we can arrange it.'

'I'm a little frightened of your big house and all that sort of thing—besides, I'm plain.'

'Are you?' He sounded astonished and she laughed. 'I think you're the most beautiful girl in the world.' He smiled down at her. 'Aunt will be delighted, and so will Corinna and Paul.'

'Mother...' said Hannah, suddenly uncertain.

'Shall have everything she wants—we'll find her a flat and see that she lives in comfort.'

'Have you a lot of money, Valentijn?'

'Yes, my darling.'

Hannah hesitated. 'I'm not sure...' she began, and was kissed into silence. 'You only have to be sure of one thing,' observed Valentijn, kissing her soundly. 'That you love me.'

'Oh, yes I do,' said Hannah. She beamed up at him through the torrents of rain, her ordinary face glowing with love and happiness. 'And I always shall.'

Turn the page for a sneak preview
of the first book in the new miniseries
DIAMONDS DOWN UNDER
from Silhouette Desire®,
VOWS & A VENGEFUL GROOM
by Bronwyn Jameson

Available January 2008

Silhouette Desire®
Always Powerful, Passionate and Provocative

Kimberley Blackstone didn't notice the waiting horde of media until it was too late. Flashbulbs exploded around her like a New Year's light show. She skidded to a halt, so abruptly her trailing suitcase all but overtook her.

This had to be a case of mistaken identity. Surely. Kimberley hadn't been on the paparazzi hit list for close to a decade, not since she'd estranged herself from her billionaire father and his headline-hungry diamond business.

But no, it was *her* name they called. *Her* face was the focus of a swarm of lenses that circled her like avid hornets. Her heart started to pound with fear-fueled adrenaline.

What did they want?

What was going on?

With a rising sense of bewilderment she scanned the crowd for a clue, and her gaze fastened on a tall, leonine figure forcing his way to the front. A tall, familiar figure. Her head came up in stunned recognition, and their gazes collided across the sea of heads before the cameras erupted with another barrage of flashes, this time right in her exposed face.

Blinded by the flashbulbs—and by the shock of that momentary eye-meet—Kimberley didn't realize his intent until he'd forged his way to her side, possibly by the sheer strength of his personality. She felt his arm wrap around her shoulder, pulling her into the protective shelter of his body, allowing her no time to object. No chance to lift her hands to ward him off.

In the space of a hastily drawn breath, she found herself plastered knee-to-nose against six feet two inches of hard-bodied male.

Ric Perrini.

Her lover for ten torrid weeks, her husband for ten tumultuous days.

Her ex for ten tranquil years.

After all this time, he should not have felt so familiar but, oh dear, he did. She knew the scent of that body and its lean, muscular strength. She knew its heat and its slick power and every response it could draw from hers.

She also recognized the ease with which he'd taken control of the moment and the decisiveness of his deep voice when it rumbled close to her ear. "I have a car waiting outside. Is this your only luggage?"

Kimberley nodded. "I assume you will tell me," she said tightly, "what this welcome party is all about."

"Not while the welcome party is within earshot. No."

Barking a request for the cameramen to stand aside, Perrini took her hand and pulled her into step with his ground-eating stride. Kimberley let him, because he was right, damn his arrogant, Italian-suited hide. Despite the speed with which he whisked her across the airport terminal, she could almost feel the hot breath of the pursuing media on her back.

This was neither the time nor the place for explanations. Inside his car, however, she would get answers.

Now that the initial shock had been blown away—by the haste of their retreat, by the heat of her gathering indignation, by the rush of adrenaline fired by Perrini's presence and the looming verbal battle—her brain was starting to tick over. This had to be her father's doing. And if it was a Howard Blackstone publicity ploy, then it had to be about Blackstone Diamonds, the company that ruled his life.

The knowledge made her chest tighten with a familiar ache of disillusionment.

She'd known her father would be flying in from Sydney for today's opening of the newest in his chain of exclusive, high-end jewelry boutiques. The opulent shopfront sat adjacent to the rival business where Kimberley worked. No coincidence, she thought bitterly, just as it was no coincidence that Ric Perrini was here in Auckland ushering her to his car.

Perrini was Howard Blackstone's right-hand man,

second in command at Blackstone Diamonds, a legacy of his short-lived marriage to the boss's daughter. No doubt her father had sent him to fetch her; the question was *why?*

* * * * *

Get swept away down under with the glitz and glamour of the Blackstone empire as Kimberley tries to determine the real reason behind her "reunion" with Ric....

Look for VOWS & A VENGEFUL GROOM by Bronwyn Jameson, in stores January 2008.

Silhouette®

Desire

When Kimberley Blackstone's father is
presumed dead, Kimberley is required to take
over the helm of Blackstone Diamonds. She
has to work closely with her ex, Ric Perrini, to
battle not only the press, but also the fierce
attraction still sizzling between them. Does Ric
feel the same...or is it the power her share of
Blackstone Diamonds will provide him as he
battles for boardroom supremacy.

Look for

VOWS &
A VENGEFUL GROOM

by

BRONWYN
JAMESON

Available January wherever you buy books

Visit Silhouette Books at www.eHarlequin.com   SD76843

Della Carlisle has hit her stride, but one
pregnancy test changes everything. The idea of
having Alexander DiRossi's baby and becoming his
traditional little housewife sends chills down Della's
spine. It takes her friends who have been there,
done that to make her see that motherhood isn't
the end of the fun, it's the beginning!

Look for

MOTHERHOOD
WITHOUT
WARNING

by

TANYA
MICHAELS

Available January wherever you buy books

HARLEQUIN®

The Next Novel.com

HN88150

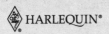
HARLEQUIN®

INTRIGUE®

INTRIGUE'S ULTIMATE HEROES

★

**6 heroes. 6 stories.
One month to read them all.**

For one special month, Harlequin Intrigue
is dedicated to those heroes among men.
Desirable doctors, sexy soldiers, brave
bodyguards—they are all
Intrigue's Ultimate Heroes.

In January, collect all 6.

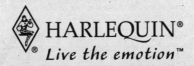
HARLEQUIN®
Live the emotion™

www.eHarlequin.com   HI69302

REQUEST YOUR FREE BOOKS!

2 FREE NOVELS PLUS 2
FREE GIFTS!

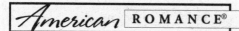

American **ROMANCE**®

Heart, Home & Happiness!

YES! Please send me 2 FREE Harlequin American Romance® novels and my 2 FREE gifts. After receiving them, if I don't wish to receive any more books, I can return the shipping statement marked "cancel." If I don't cancel, I will receive 4 brand-new novels every month and be billed just $4.24 per book in the U.S., or $4.99 per book in Canada, plus 25¢ shipping and handling per book and applicable taxes, if any*. That's a savings of close to 15% off the cover price! I understand that accepting the 2 free books and gifts places me under no obligation to buy anything. I can always return a shipment and cancel at any time. Even if I never buy another book from Harlequin, the two free books and gifts are mine to keep forever.

154 HDN EEZK   354 HDN EEZV

Name	(PLEASE PRINT)

Address	Apt. #

City	State/Prov.	Zip/Postal Code

Signature (if under 18, a parent or guardian must sign)

Mail to the **Harlequin Reader Service**®:
IN U.S.A.: P.O. Box 1867, Buffalo, NY 14240-1867
IN CANADA: P.O. Box 609, Fort Erie, Ontario L2A 5X3

Not valid to current Harlequin American Romance subscribers.

Want to try two free books from another line?
Call 1-800-873-8635 or visit www.morefreebooks.com.

* Terms and prices subject to change without notice. NY residents add applicable sales tax. Canadian residents will be charged applicable provincial taxes and GST. This offer is limited to one order per household. All orders subject to approval. Credit or debit balances in a customer's account(s) may be offset by any other outstanding balance owed by or to the customer. Please allow 4 to 6 weeks for delivery.

Your Privacy: Harlequin is committed to protecting your privacy. Our Privacy Policy is available online at www.eHarlequin.com or upon request from the Reader Service. From time to time we make our lists of customers available to reputable firms who may have a product or service of interest to you. If you would prefer we not share your name and address, please check here. ☐

HAR07

Inside ROMANCE

Stay up-to-date on all your romance reading news!

Inside Romance is a FREE quarterly newsletter highlighting our upcoming series releases and promotions.

Visit

www.eHarlequin.com/InsideRomance

to sign up to receive our complimentary newsletter today!

IRNJ1107

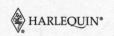

EVERLASTING LOVE™

Every great love has a story to tell™

Rabble-rousing East Coast hippie Zoe Wingfield and levelheaded Wisconsin farm boy Spencer Andersen couldn't have been more wrong for each other. Yet their bond when they met was instant. It has sustained them through forty years of wars and personal crises. Will it hold for their most difficult challenge of all?

Look for

This Side of Heaven

by

Anna Schmidt

Available January wherever you buy books.

www.eHarlequin.com

HEL65425

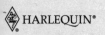

EVERLASTING LOVE™

Every great love has a story to tell™

Nick and Stefanie Marsden met in
high school, fell in love and married
four years later. But thirty years later,
when Nick goes missing, everything—
love and life itself—hangs in the balance
during this long winter night. A night of
memories. A night of hope and faith…

Look for

by

Rebecca Winters

Available January wherever you buy books.

www.eHarlequin.com

HEL65426

SPECIAL EDITION™

INTRODUCING A NEW 6-BOOK MINISERIES!

THE WILDER FAMILY
Healing Hearts in Walnut River

Walnut River's most prominent family,
the Wilders, are reunited in their struggle to
stop their small hospital from being taken over
by a medical conglomerate. Not only do they
find their family bonds again, they also find love.

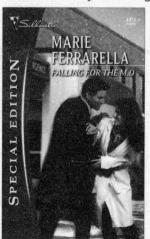

STARTING WITH

FALLING FOR THE M.D.

by *USA TODAY*
bestselling author

MARIE FERRARELLA

January 2008

*Look for a book from The Wilder Family
every month until June!*

Visit Silhouette Books at www.eHarlequin.com   SSE24873